THE SUBMARINER

The Submariner

Edward Stephens

1973

DOUBLEDAY & COMPANY, INC.
GARDEN CITY, NEW YORK

ISBN: 0-385-08884-1
Library of Congress Catalog Card Number 73-79715
Copyright © 1973 by Edward Stephens
Printed in the United States of America
First Edition

For Ken McCormick

If the slayer thinks he slays,
If the slain thinks he is slain,
Both these do not understand:
He slays not, is not slain.

Katha Upanishad 2.19

THE SUBMARINER

1

SECOND NUCLEAR SUBMARINE LOST AT SEA! the headline in the Washington *Post* said.

The rear admiral glanced through the story and put the paper down on his desk. He drained his coffeecup and finished his cigarette standing before the great wall chart of the Caribbean Sea, the Straits of Florida, and the Gulf of Mexico. His aide came in with the papers.

"Morning, Admiral."

"Well," the admiral said. "D Day, H Hour, eh?"

"Yes, sir, Admiral," the aide said, already moving to fall in step with the rear admiral. Swiftly they traversed the E ring, looking out for the bicycles moving along the corridors with the mail. When they reached the office of the Chief of Naval Operations, the rear admiral took the papers from the aide and said, "Thanks. See you back in the office." Then, driven by some vagrant whim, a slight suggestion of sullenness in the aide's expression, or possibly a tag end of some unpurged uncertainty of his own, the rear admiral said,

"Wait. You were at the meetings, you've seen the scenario, read my memorandum. This is the right thing I am recommending, don't you think? The only sensible course?"

"I—I'd rather not say, Admiral."

"Speak up, Commander. I'm waiting."

"No, sir."

"What?"

"I don't think it is. I think Commodore Forbes is right, sir. Even if we managed to—"

"Oh, check my calendar, will you? Make sure my secretary canceled anything I have for the next couple of hours. And make the usual arrangements for lunch. That's all."

The aide said, Aye, aye, sir, possibly even saluting, but the rear admiral had turned away, dismissing him not only from his mind but from his employ and protection. The aide would be on an oiler in WestPac in five days.

CNO had a regular fleet of secretaries, aides, and assorted sailors deployed in a defensive perimeter among the desks and machinery of his outer office, but they all knew the rear admiral and he was expected and he walked right in exuding confidence and commandpresence the way a movie star exudes sex appeal.

"Hello, Jim," CNO said, extending from an incredible array of heavy gold braid a tanned seaman's hand, hard and firm. Glistening teeth flashed against the tanned and rugged face. He might have stepped off the flag bridge of a carrier, though in the last few years he had spent more time on the golf course than he had at sea.

"Good morning, Admiral," the rear admiral said. "Thank you for seeing me so promptly."

"Have a seat. Coffee?"

"You know me and coffee, Admiral."

"I never should have asked."

They shared businessmen's laughter, born not of amusement but of camaraderie, virility, companion to the firm handclasp, the steadygaze, the ritual reference to family and friends sipping the hot strong coffee in delicate chinacups bluecrested with four stars, mess stewards in white rustling out the door, carefully closing it signaling the end of the preamble and the beginning of business. But CNO, epitome of grace and tact, refused to be abrupt.

"And young Jimmie? How is your boy getting along at the Academy?"

"Just commissioned, sir. Stood one in his class, I am proud to say. Accepted for nuclear-power school. Just happen to have some pictures of him here."

"So he will be a submariner like his old man."

"Right into the nuclear program. Navy of the future. Ground floor. Skip the old diesel boats completely."

"You made quite a record in the old diesel boats, Jim."

"This is him with his fiancée, Mary Beth. Isn't she a beauty? Sweet as she is pretty. Fine family. Her father is an army lieutenant general. They'll be married when he makes j.g. I thought it best to wait until he had his first sea duty behind him. I couldn't be happier."

"You want to remember that he's the one that's marrying her."

"Oh, he couldn't be happier either."

"Jim—you're up for promotion to vice admiral with the next selection board. I don't think there will be any problem. As soon as you are selected I believe I can promise you a major fleet command. I know that's what you've been wanting, and of course it's the right move toward making your own fourth star down the road. Possibly the first fleet, or the seventh."

"Thank you, Admiral. I imagine the most important part of that would be I'd at least rank my son's father-in-law. Knowing Mary Beth, that'll be important."

They shared more laughter, warm, polite, but moderating. Time for business now. The rear admiral stuck a cigarette in his ivory holder and lighted it speaking through smoke and the snap of his Zippo (chromium, engraved, a gift from some grateful crew).

"Admiral, we have got to take decisive action to stop this threat to our nuclear submarine fleet."

CNO's expression and voice changed, lost their air of friendly exchange as he became once again the senior officer in the U. S. Navy being petitioned by a subordinate.

"I have studied your memorandum. You make quite a persuasive case—"

"Then you will do it, sir?"

"I can hardly give you official permission to start World War III, Jim. You know that."

"You see the story in the *Post* this morning? I should have brought it along."

"I've seen it."

"They say if we've lost two nukes through some kind of accident it proves we don't know how to build them right. So Congress ought to cut back on our appropriation for nuclear submarine construction. Why they quote some senator in there as saying the whole nuclear program ought to be scrapped."

"I know. The New York *Times* is whistling the same tune."

"You know as well as I do, Admiral—those ships were sunk by enemy action."

CNO looked away toward the huge chart of the world's waterways which filled one complete wall. He sighed.

"I know it. And you know it. I've seen some intelligence even you haven't seen yet and I'm convinced our submarines were sunk by an enemy submarine, submerged, so it would look like an accident."

"An enemy nuke. Lies in wait submerged, then"—the rear admiral moved his finger through the air, cocking the thumb—"*bang!* . . . fish in a rain barrel. Just like that. And nobody the wiser."

"What to do about it, that's the question."

"My memorandum, sir. Do unto others as they have done unto you. An eye for an eye, a submarine for a submarine. Submerged. And nobody the wiser."

"Jim, our nuclear submarines are under the control of the Congress. Every movement has to be cleared in advance with the Armed Forces Committee. Not only that, every senator and congressman and staffer in the White House wants to take a ride in one. Our nukes are showboats. It's going to be a long time before they are just routine operating elements of the fleet. Even if they were, I'd need approval of the Congress before I started a war."

"You wouldn't be starting one, you'd be stopping one."

"That enemy submarine is Russian."

"Nobody would know."

"God damn it, I am trying to tell you. The Congress would know. You read the papers. You see the *Congressional Record*. My God, we've got senators who would—"

"Admiral, you might possibly, considering the extraordinarily sensitive nature of this situation, might possibly consider taking the matter directly to the President in his capacity as Commander in Chief. Sidestepping the Congress."

"I did just that."

"What did he say?"

"He said what I just said. He can't say yes."

"Well, if he means—"

"I am not going to go into what he means or doesn't mean. That is what he said."

"But, Admiral, if he said no I don't—"

"You didn't hear me."

"Sir?"

"I said he didn't say yes."

CNO sat absolutely immobile, looking at the rear admiral, the rear admiral looking back at him, two men well past the middle years in blue suits with gold lace on the sleeves seated in heavy leather chairs over coffee in delicate chinacups discussing this matter as, in other offices in other parts of the nation, other men discussed the design of automobiles or the sale of soap.

"I see," the rear admiral said.

"Do you, Jim? May we speak hypothetically? If you were going to go about such a thing as you propose, how would you go about it? Get around the publicity, the Congress and all the attendant glare and complications?"

"A diesel submarine, sir."

"A *diesel?*"

"They are under the operational control of the squadron commanders. Their deployment originates with officers operating under my delegated authority. It doesn't have to be approved at a level higher than mine."

CNO looked again at the vast wall chart, looked back at the rear admiral. "Nuclear weapons would be absolutely out of the question."

"Yes, sir. A regular old-fashioned Mark 14 steam fish. Possibly an acoustic torpedo with a regulation warhead if I can scrape one up—accountability might be a bit of a problem. But nothing fancy. No nuclear debris in the water."

"Assuming her reactor is sufficiently shielded when she goes down."

"Well, ours were. That's another reason to move very fast on this. If by chance she did put some nuclear waste in the water, it could always have come from our own nuclear losses."

"We have already announced there was none."

"We could have been wrong."

"The diesel submarine—there would seem to be a certain expendability involved."

"Which of course is another excellent reason for using a diesel boat, sir. We can spare one. We are already phasing them out."

"How about Sam Greice in the *Starfish?*"

"He'd be a good one to sacrifice, all right, but that's a New London boat and this guy we're after seems to operate around the Caribbean and the Gulf."

"So you see it as a sacrifice?"

"I shouldn't have said that."

"But you do."

"To head off a third world war—that's hardly a sacrifice. It's a duty."

"Would you by any chance have a particular submarine in mind?"

"Commodore Forbes has a boat in his squadron down in Key West that has been unsat in its last three ORI's. Quite a headache because of her discipline and morale problems, and a lot of other things."

"Highly unusual in the submarine force, I must say."

"Unusual and unfortunate, but it can happen in any organization. A unit gets a bad reputation and then everything conspires to make it worse. All the good people put in to get off, and the other ships send their bad apples to her. Men who have really fouled up somewhere else get sent to her to get them out of the way. In this single respect the *Devilfish* is absolutely outstanding. Forbes says they have crewmen on there who already rate a BCD which is suspended on the condition, unofficial of course, that they serve on the *Devilfish*. It's the only way they can get crew enough to man her. As it is she's terribly shorthanded. She's only in commission at all because our authorized strength requires it. If we hadn't had these losses, she'd already be scrap iron." The rear admiral lighted another cigarette, snapped his Zippo shut. "Let me put it this way. It's the sort of boat which if my son went to it, I'd rather see him resign his commission. Bunch of bums is all. The Navy has a few, even the submarine force. They are all on that boat. In a way I suppose she is a product of our times."

"You sound like one of those sociologists the government has been sending around."

"If the government would give us more money for upkeep and recruiting, and fewer sociologists, we wouldn't have boats like the *Devilfish*. At least now we can put her to good use."

"Forbes could get caught in the middle on something like this. How does he feel about it?"

The rear admiral shrugged. "He is opposed."

"You would go around him?"

"He is merely a subordinate squadron commodore."

"He could catch the brunt of it if anything went wrong."

The rear admiral stubbed out his cigarette poking the ivory holder in the ash tray, flicking out the stub with his little finger. "He would have the satisfaction of knowing he had helped save the nation from disaster."

CNO studied him as their coffeecups were refilled.

"This would seem to be a job for our best crew, Jim. Not our worst."

"They are troublemakers and misfits, sir, but not necessarily incompetent seamen. In fact, the skipper is Orin Feldman."

"Feldman? I thought he got out long ago."

"Well, he went to the *Devilfish*. Same thing."

"I see."

"His troubles were, are, uh, nonmilitary."

"My God," CNO said. "That whole thing from the

Naval Academy—the girl and everything—it ended up down there in Key West?"

"On the *Devilfish.*"

"Murphy too?"

"The three of them."

"What was her name?"

"Jacqueline."

"Didn't—wasn't—" CNO stopped himself in midphrase, looking hard at the rear admiral through opaque eyes suddenly clouded, and then he lifted the sleeve with the heavy layers of gold braid and touched the rear admiral's gold-braided sleeve and said, "I'm sorry, Jim. I didn't mean to—"

"That's okay, sir. Okay. That was some time ago. Doesn't matter. Has nothing to do with this, of course."

"Of course. Well," briskly, rising, looking at his watch, already moving, the rear admiral moving automatically with him, putting down his coffeecup, picking up his papers, putting his cigaretteholder in his pocket.

They were at the door of the inner office.

"Good of you to come by, Jim. I'm sorry we couldn't approve your plan."

"At least you didn't turn it down."

The two admirals stood in their blue suits with the gold braid running down along the forearms heavy and richly glowing. Their eyes locked, one brain looking into the other.

"I can tell you exactly what the President said, Jim."

"Yes, sir?"

CNO put one hand in one jacket pocket and shifted his gaze a little, looking just over the rear admiral's blue shoulder.

"He said, 'A man would have to be a damn fool to approve a plan like that.'"

"I see. Is that all he said, sir?"

"Why, no. No, it isn't. He said something else."

"And what was that?"

CNO looked back into the rear admiral's eyes. "Why, he said, 'If anybody was fool enough to pull off a stunt like that I wouldn't want to know a damn thing about it because if I did I would have to present his nuts to Congress in a little velvet box.'"

"The President is given to vigorous speech."

"He is nobody's fool, Jimmie. Don't forget that."

"I'll keep it in mind, Admiral."

"Keep everything in mind, Jim. Or on the scrambler phone. Nothing in writing. Nothing. And it has got to be neat. If it isn't, it's World War III. And they will name it after you."

2

The ensign awakened with a headache. In T shirt and
shorts he went forward to the head. He opened the door
and there seated on the john was an incredible creature
who finally the ensign staring open-mouthed realized was
one of the women from the Havana Madrid. She had on
the same dress which was now drawn up around her
scrawny thighs.

"Be out in a minute, honey," she said in a low, crackly
voice, the eyes distant and dull, enlivened by a kind of
reddish inflammation, traces of matter visible at the corners. If she had looked bad last night in the flattering
light of the bar, she was a full-blown specter in the head's
bright light, hair a tangled mop, make-up congealed in
crazy splotches and swirls, lipstick spread faintly from
chin to nose and up toward one ear. An effluvium of
stale liquor filled the little cubicle.

When the ensign just stood staring, she said, "Know
where I can get a cup of coffee, honey?"

Abruptly the ensign remembered last night, but it only
made his head hurt more. He had reported to the submarine yesterday but there was no one aboard. Just the
duty officer, a fat j.g., so old he had to be a mustang, lying
on his bunk in a frayed old bathrobe and carpet slippers,
reading the newspaper, and a few sailors hanging around

loafing as other men in other times and places might loaf around the pool hall in the bad part of town. There was no duty section, no below-decks watch, no topside watch to salute him and welcome him aboard and log him in. Just the rusty submarine with the derelicts hanging around.

"Is this vessel actually in commission?" he had asked the fat mustang, who wouldn't even get out of his bunk.

"Why? Who the hell wants to know?"

"I am trying to report aboard. I wish to log in properly, in accordance with regulations. Will you—"

"No. I'm busy." A passing sailor guffawed loudly, broken teeth showing.

"Hey!" the ensign said. "He has a can of beer. He can't—"

"Go grab him and take it away from him if you want it."

"Where is the executive officer?"

"Miami, I think."

"Then where is the captain?"

"Home, I suppose. This time of night."

"It's only twenty hundred hours."

"Very nautical. You must be from the Naval Academy."

"I am going directly to the captain."

The mustang didn't answer him.

"What is the captain's address?"

"Santa Maria Motel."

"You mean he lives there? In a motel?"

"Well, he eats and sleeps there and takes an occasional leak. I suppose you'd call that living there. You might ask him. Go ahead right on over. Probably invite you for dinner."

"Fine. Now who can I give my orders to?"

"I don't know. Give 'em to the captain."

"Who is the chief of the boat?"

"Sprague, I suppose."

"Where is he?"

"Beach."

"Where on the beach?"

"That twenty hunnert hours shit. What's that mean?"

"You serious? You don't know what that means?"

"I'm asking you do you know what it means."

"Eight o'clock P.M."

"Then he'd be at the Havana Madrid."

"That another motel?"

The mustang just looked at him then back at his newspaper which he read listlessly, moving his lips slightly.

"I will see the captain and leave my card, then check in with Chief Sprague and leave my orders. I must say this is a most unusual way to run a submarine."

"How would you know? You ever been aboard one?"

"No, but I have studied shipboard organization and—"

"No, *sir*, when you talk to me, you little shit. You are in the presence of a superior officer. Show a little respect or I'll put you on report. I seen a copy of your orders. I don't care who your daddy is, Junior. Now get the hell out of my sight."

A fleshy woman, completely nude, stood gyrating on the open-air stage as the ensign entered the Havana Madrid.

"This isn't a motel at all," he said to the bartender. "It's a bar."

"You'll make admiral in a hurry, Ensign. Way you size things up like that. You old enough to be in here? Lemme see your I.D. card—"

"I am not here socially. I am here on business. Would you happen to know a Chief Sprague?"

"At's Sprague over there." He indicated with his chin and cigarette a square-shaped sailor in whites just then with his hand on the breast of a skinny woman standing by his barstool.

"No, I'm looking for a chief."

"Well, that's Sprague. Only one of him, thank God. Come to think of it, he might of been a chief once along the line . . ."

During the subsequent four or five hours as the ensign tried to chastise Sprague and straighten him out

(*"You can't be the chief of the boat, you're only a first-class—"*

(*"Take it up with the exec."*

(*"Where is he?"*

(*"Who knows? Fort Lauderdale maybe. Depends where Jackie is."*

(*"Jackie? Jackie? Isn't that the captain's wife's name? I just saw her."*

(*"Where?"*

(*"At the motel."*

(*"Orin there?"*

(*"Who?"*

(*"The captain."*

(*"No."*

(*"She alone?"*

(*"No."*

(*"That was Jackie."*

(*"Well, it's none of my business."*

(*"Betcher sweet ass. Better buy us a drink."*)

he found it impossible to avoid consuming (he did not drink) several jiggers of cheap bourbon surreptitiously added to the ginger ale he relentlessly ordered and consumed while trying to find out he could not remember what from Sprague, who did not seem to care.

Now his head hurt as he stood shouting at the woman in the head, "Get off this vessel!" while her eyes traveled to his gaping shorts and back to his face.

"You're kinda cute, honey—"

"I said get off this vessel *now* or I will—"

"Okay, okay, that's what I'm trying to do, honey. But your buddy over there ain't much help. Now close the door and let a girl finish up. Kinda place is this, anyway?"

The ensign turned to where she had nodded. There in one of the lower bunks an anthropoid figure lay, one thick arm dangling over and onto the deck. He lay face down clad in a skivvyshirt and nothing else, emitting now a faint liquid snore. On the deck beside his hand an empty whiskey bottle stood surrounded by crumpled cigarette packages, matchbooks, small change, a comb, lipstick, nylon stockings, sailorpants, an overflowing ash tray.

"Sprague!" the ensign shouted. "Sprague! Get up! Get up and—and—" Sprague only spluttered and turned his head to a more comfortable position against the back of his hand.

The ensign shook him savagely until finally he cocked his head up blearily. "What the hell—"

"Sprague! This is a court-martial offense. Get that— that *woman* off this ship *at once!*"

"Whaaa—?"

"There! Her!" The woman was emerging from the head, giving them a ghastly grin.

"Oh Jesus," Sprague said. He reached beneath the thin mattresspad where no matter what else he had done or not done he had remembered with the wisdom of experience to hide his wallet. One cheek was bloody, the other was covered with lipstick. He tossed some bills at the ensign's feet.

"Call her a cab," he said and put his head down and began at once to snore again.

The ensign turned and stepped through the watertight door and went to the wardroom where the mustang, Lieutenant (j.g.) Foster, who had the duty, sat in domestic content, in his pajamas, reading the morning paper over coffee and sweet rolls.

Standing stiffly at attention in the passageway, the ensign knocked on the bulkhead beside the wardroom entrance. The mustang glanced up and back at his paper.

"What the hell do you want me to get your coffee for you too?" He jerked his thumb over his shoulder. "Help yourself."

"Mr. Foster—there is a woman aboard!"

The mustang stopped his coffeecup in its arc, blew thoughtfully over the steaming surface. "Is that a actual fact, Junior?"

"Mr. Foster, this is no laughing matter."

"I ain't laughing, kid." He turned a page, lips pursed, eyes squinted, following a story, sipping his coffee. There was an air of contented homeliness about him that infuriated the ensign.

"Mr. Foster, I repeat, there is a woman aboard this submarine. She spent the night here *with a member of the crew!* If you refuse to take any action I shall have to inform the captain personally of your dereliction."

"Don't yell at me. She didn't spend the night with me. In fact, just shut up."

"What's all the noise about?"

It was the executive officer, standing in the doorway. He was a tall and remarkably handsome man with thick black hair neatly combed. He wore a crisp khaki shirt with the twin silver lieutenant's bars at each collarpoint, a black knit nonregulation necktie and freshly pressed khaki-colored gabardine trousers. He smelled of rich shaving cologne. He stood in the passageway, his immaculate hat in one hand, the other hand holding the cigarette, the fingers rubbing his cheek and his chin.

"The ensign here has a complaint," the mustang said, examining now with interest the ensign who stood in a stiff military brace, eyes straight ahead, thumbs at the seams of his skivvyshorts, hair tousled, unshaven chin tucked in to the top of his wrinkled T shirt, bare toes curled up away from the cold steel deck.

"What about?" the executive officer said.

"I guess he ought to tell you. Go ahead, kid."

"Well, sir—"

"Burt, Jackie's still asleep. You might have Martinez take her some coffee in a while. That today's paper?"

"Yesterday's."

"She likes today's paper and she's out of cigarettes. Junior, my car is up on the dock. How about running up —aw, never mind, you aren't even dressed." He glanced at his watch and back at the ensign. "Kind of late to be standing around like that, isn't it? I'll do it myself along the way. You want anything, Burt?"

"Cigarettes." The mustang's bully voice took on abruptly a boot seaman's whine. "I had the duty last night and I got it again today and I had it last time we was in port. It just ain't fair and Martinez is—"

"How about you, Junior? Smokes?"

"I don't smoke, sir."

"Tell him what you was telling me," the mustang said.

"Could it possibly wait till I get back?" the executive officer said. "I'm on my way to see the commodore."

"Yessir."

The executive officer left. His glistening brown shoes had leather heels and the ensign listened to their military clickclack as he walked forward and stepped over the coaming and into the forward torpedo room and stopped.

"Good," the ensign said. "Now we'll just see about all of this . . ."

But all he heard was the unintelligible sound of low voices, then the footsteps again and finally the opening and closing of the torpedo room hatch.

"Take her her coffee now, kid."

"I most certainly will not."

"Listen, Junior. I don't give a damn who you are. When you're aboard this boat you obey orders from your superior officers. That's me. Move your ass."

The ensign stood staring. Then he padded over to the Silex and poured a cup of coffee and went out into the passageway and turned left.

"Where you going? She's the other way."

"No. She's—"

"In the capm's stateroom, for God's sake. Don't you even know where that is?"

The ensign stopped, balancing the coffee. "There must be two women aboard, then."

"Fantastic. Simply amazing. They teach you to reason like that at the Naval Academy?"

Lieutenant (j.g.) Foster was bald-headed, short and round. He was a mustang who had worked his way up through all the enlisted ranks until, after thirty-five years in the Navy, the last five as a chief petty officer, he had been commissioned a lieutenant (j.g.). Nobody, including him, knew exactly why. He was the oldest officer aboard the submarine while also the most junior—or had been until the ensign reported aboard. The ensign was the first officer to whom the mustang had ever given an order.

"*Git!*" the mustang cried suddenly. "Goddam it, you little shit, don't you ever just stand there after I have give you a direct command!"

Only to j.g.'s are j.g.'s senior enough to order ensigns around like that, but the ensign did not understand that yet. At the Naval Academy j.g.'s were celebrities. So the ensign jumped, spilling hot coffee on his bare foot, jumping again, spilling more.

He went down the passageway to the captain's stateroom and stood staring at the drawn curtain. He smelled perfume, an incongruous fragrance here in the submarine. He knocked beside the green curtain.

"Harold?"

"It's me. Ensign Hillerby."

"Who? *Oh.* You left your card last night. Come in."

He pulled the curtain. The first thing he saw was her bare back. She had the harness of her bra on but the strap was not fastened. Her pale yellow hair, the color of straw, fell lightly over her shoulders.

"Hook me up, will you?"

"*Me?*"

She looked around. He saw quite clearly the swelling bosom. "Who else? Oh. Don't you look *cute.*"

"Ex-*cuse* me—"

He tried to leave, but she insisted, all insouciance, holding the straps back toward him. So he put the coffee on the fold-down desk and tried to get his fingers to cooperate. He had once furtively squirming unhooked Mary Beth's bra, but this was the first one he had ever hooked (Mary Beth, sullen with accusation, had rehooked her own) and standing up in the light and the captain's wife and him in shorts at that.

The hooks and eyes were small, intricate affairs and he was trembling, his fingers jerking and twitching. It was only when he had finished ("There, that'll do it," trying to sound hearty, match her insouciance, but his voice betrayed him) that he realized she had been watching him in the mirror on the medicine chest over the basin, smiling. Her fragrance made it hard to breathe, her closeness.

Then she was drawing a yellow cashmere sweater over her head elevating her arms, her armpits graceful hollows cleanshaven and smooth.

"I stood one in my class," he blurted. "They gave me a sword."

She studied him frankly: face, bare feet, knees, bulgy skivvyshorts, smiling, touching her hair.

"I see you're wearing it."

She was moving then through the doorway into the passageway. She wore open-toed sandals with high heels. Her toenails were pink. Mesmerized, he followed, admiring her white legs as, elevating her skirt, she stepped over the coaming into the forward torpedo room.

Then he remembered what was up there. He sprinted forward. The creature from the Havana Madrid was gone. Sprague was still in the bunk, on his back now, snoring loudly: somebody had pulled a light blanket over him. She was standing looking down at Sprague, at where the blanket thrust up like a tentpole.

"He's not supposed to be there!" the ensign shouted. "He is supposed to be up."

"Looks like he is up all right," she said and leaned over and curled her middle finger against her thumb and went *flick!* hard against the tentpole, admiring the way it deflated as Sprague snorted in discomfort and began to awaken.

"Now he can roll over," she said moving to the ladder which went up into the hatch, climbing easily up.

"Wait!" the ensign called inanely, running after her, stumbling, catching up. "It's hot out. You better stay—"

"I'm air-conditioned," she said. She kept on going up the ladder, turning then to stand in the escape trunk, looking down at him.

"What?" he cried. "You're—"

"The car. The motel. Listen—"

"What?"

"Tell Harold I've gone on back."

Hands over her head she turned the dogging wheel and the heavy spring lifted the hatch cover and her white legs disappeared into the dazzling sunlight.

The ensign found the mustang standing beside him, looking up. He had a funny look on his face.

"You say one word," the ensign said, "and I'll bust your nose."

But the mustang didn't say anything.

3

They sailed that afternoon for Havana, the ensign protesting and complaining as they maneuvered away from the piers and made for the channel. He hadn't had time to do this, he hadn't had time to do that.

"I'm supposed to get ready to go to submarine school, I'm not supposed to be ship's company yet."

"We're awfully short-handed right now," the executive officer said. "We'll send you later. Right now you are assistant navigator and assistant operations officer."

"But I've never—"

The executive officer calling orders to the helm cut him short. "You been studying for four years at the Naval Academy haven't you? You must have learned *something*. You must be good for *something*."

"Who is the navigator, sir? Who do I report to then?"

"He's not aboard. Didn't make it."

"The navigator missed the ship? That's impossible."

"That's the kind of navigator he is. It's no loss. We're just as well off—even with you."

"I better get below and check the charts."

"You do that. Find Sprague, the first-class quartermaster."

The ensign went below. There was no one in the conning tower but the helmsman, a young sailor with a badly scarred face. "Where is the quartermaster of the watch?"

"Sprague? Down taking a leak."

"He is supposed to be up here on duty."

The helmsman turned around to look at him. "Well, he can't very well take a leak up here can he?"

"Mind your helm."

"Mind your own business."

"What's your name?"

"I forget."

"You're on report, sailor. What's your name?"

"Bull Halsey."

The ensign got out his notebook. "Bull what?"

"Bull shit." The sailor turned back to his wheel, his compass, his coffee and cigarette, flicking an ash heavily with his thumb.

The ensign went to the chart table in the after corner of the conning tower. Everything was very neat and orderly, the channel chart taped down and the sortie track laid off, course changes for the doglegs neatly penciled in. The ensign studied the chart intently for a while, then went back up on the bridge and stood stiffly beside the executive officer.

They both wore khaki. The ensign's was new, still showing the store creases. The executive officer's was worn smooth from countless washings and so faded it seemed in the brilliant sun almost white. His shirt and trousers were immaculate, starched to razoredges so that occasionally when he moved he rustled. His shirt was open five or six buttons, almost to his waist, and he was hatless. He wore no T shirt. The left hand on the binoculars bore the heavy Academy class ring with an onyx stone.

The ensign loosened his tie and unbuttoned his shirt a button or so at a time until he emulated the executive officer, telling himself it was cooler. His open shirt exposed to the elements his regulation smallstores T shirt of heavy white cotton. He wore the shiny visor of his new officer's cap low over his eyes. When they got to the first dogleg the ensign barked out a number.

"What's that?" the executive officer said.

"The course to the next turn, sir."

As they approached each dogleg in the channel the ensign would announce the new course and the executive officer would only stare out over the bow and maybe grunt. The submarine would turn and steady on the new course and in a while the ensign would announce the new course coming up.

"You sure as hell make a lot of noise," the executive officer said.

"Sir! Mr. Murphy, sir—"

"Yeah?"

"How did you do that? Rounding the channel marker just like that, a perfect turn, without any course or any orders to the helm or anything?"

The executive officer was looking through his binoculars. "I got her in automatic, Junior."

The sea was endless, vast and blue, like nothing the ensign had ever seen before. It was translucent, admitting and diffusing light so completely that the entire element in which the submarine rode seemed unreal, an airy fantasy of crystal blue and yellowish white.

The channel markers drifted by to starboard numbered neat and orderly, their cables clearly visible slanting down like dark threads in the lightblue fabric of the sea. At every dogleg in the tortuous channel the submarine turned smartly with full rudder then settled on the new course to the next. The executive officer seemed a passenger, though when the ensign finally noticed a submarine approaching around the next buoy he found the executive officer already studying it through his binoculars.

"Should I pass the word, sir? Assemble all hands for rendering or receiving honors up on the forecastle and on the after deck sir?"

"No."

"I mean, of course first I'll look up the signal number of the commanding officer of the approaching ship so we will know who renders honors to whom. And who receives. If you would just read off the hull number I'll get the book and—"

"Relax, Junior. You're not in school any more."

"But, sir, tradition and regulations *require* that U.S. naval vessels passing at sea render proper and appropriate honors and salutes with music if appropriate."

"Yeah? Well you might whistle us a tune, Junior. Something martial."

"I'll get the book, sir, then we can—"

"You don't need any book. That's Spunky Waters' boat. Hey! On the wheel! Come left five."

"Left five, aye!" came up the hatch.

"Crank her up to full."

"Full, aye."

From the dark circle of the open hatch bells jangled. The deck throbbed as the engines revved up. The approaching submarine developed a bone in her teeth too, and just before her bow swung toward them there was the plume of white water aft, indicating her own increased speed. The distance began rapidly to close.

"Mr. Murphy!" the ensign bawled. "Mr. Murphy! You better come right sir! We're heading right for him."

"Nah. He's heading for us."

The executive officer seemed faintly interested for the first time since they had left the dock. He rode now leaning against the cowl, hands in his pockets, squinting into the wind. He seemed to be sighting along the length of the bow, estimating just where they would hit.

"Mr. Murphy—"

But the executive officer was calling calmly down the hatch. "Give me two more to the left."

"Left?" the ensign cried. "Not left—"

"Why?" came up the hatch at once.

"See?" the ensign shouted. "Even the helmsman is—"

He was interrupted by the executive officer's hard grip on his arm, moving him abruptly aside, away from the hatch.

"Little game of chicken of the sea," the executive officer called down. "You got him in the scope?"

"Who is it?" came up. A new voice: Sprague's whiskey growl.

"Spunky Waters."

"Oh, him."

"Shave his ass."

"Shavesass, aye."

Upon which the executive officer became a spectator, chin forwardthrust, hands in the starched and crackling pockets, shoulder forward over the bridge cowl. The binoculars, forgotten, swung from his neck and banged against the metal.

The submarines headed directly for one another in the center of the channel, very little room to maneuver. Now the ensign could see quite clearly the O.O.D. on the other submarine standing on the bridge, and above and behind him, standing up on the turtleback with his arms spread wide to grasp the handholds, another officer in a tie and cap. They were so close the ensign could see the scrambled eggs on the visor.

"That man is a commander!" the ensign cried.

"That's Spunky himself. Personal appearance. An honor. Don't forget to whistle at him."

"Collision stations!" the ensign screamed. "Collision—" and reached for the red handle of the bridge collision alarm.

The executive officer grabbed his wrist without even looking at him, staring transfixed across the narrowing strip of water.

"Aren't you going to do something?"

"But that's the game, Junior. He has to do it. Don't you see? Where's your sporting blood?"

"Game?" the ensign said. "You really—"

"Chicken of the sea." The executive officer made a sound that may have been laughter though his face did not show it. "See who's chicken."

"He's not going to change course!" the ensign cried, screamed, his voice high-pitched and raw in the wind.

"Sure he will. Spunky always does. Spunky is the original chicken of the sea. That's why he's a commander and wears chicken shit on his hat."

The executive officer dropped into a pocket of time and space all his own, profound, inviolable, very keen and alert and absolutely relaxed. His mouth was open a little and his eyes were very bright. The ensign was jabbing his shoulder but the executive officer had forgotten him again.

The ensign climbed up and over the cowl and got up onto the turtleback and stood with one leg out, calculating his chances of leaping over the tank tops and hitting the water safely. He was just about to let go and shove out when he was arrested by the sound of a semihuman voice screaming invective across the water. It was the CO of the other submarine jumping up and down, waving one fist and then the other (carefully hanging on), a man possessed. His submarine began to change course to its right. Just a careful few degrees.

"He isn't changing course enough!" the ensign shouted. "He should put the helm hard over!"

"Relax, Junior. Spunky's just yellow, not dumb. If he put any more helm on her his stern would slide right on over into my bow."

"I forgot about that."

"You want to be glad Spunky didn't."

They passed port to port no more than ten feet between them. They rode each through the other's bow wave and the turbulence rolled the submarines fiercely this way and that and for one terrible second the upper parts of the shears with all the exposed and vulnerable gear seemed to brush.

"—ksucker!" the other captain was shouting. They could see him quite clearly, his face contorted, fist shaking. His hat had blown off. "—nuvabitchinassole! Crazy no-good motherf—"

"Don't be a sore loser, Spunky!"

And then they were in each other's wake, spray coming over peculiarly warm, the deck corkscrewing slightly.

"All ahead two thirds," the executive officer said down the hatch. "Kee-rist, Sprague, that was beautiful. Congratulations."

Bells jangled in the conning tower. The submarine slowed, wallowed down a little. The only reminder of the contest was the odd pattern of their wakes already fading, merging as everything must into the infinite sea.

After a while the executive officer said, "See that up there, Junior? That's the sea buoy. I'm going below."

He dropped down the hatch and disappeared. The sea buoy rode by on a crest, slick with seaspray and beyond it only the trackless sea. Now the buoy bit more eagerly into

the ocean's stately roll. The ensign squinted against the
wind and spray and sunglare. He tried to think of a command to give, could think of none. There were no other
ships in sight. He thought of Mary Beth, how proud she
would be, how impressed that he was standing his first
O.O.D. watch so soon. He tried to stay alert. Mary Beth
said her father thought young Navy officers had a pretty
easy time of it.

The ensign was on the bridge a long time. There were
occasional ships. All he did was look at them as Sprague's
whiskey voice came up the hatch, "He'll pass well clear to
port," or to starboard or astern. At first the ensign said
"How far?" but after a while he quit asking even that. He
was very tired, and the emerald sea was endless.

Hypnotized by the bow wave showing now some phosphorescence, the ensign was startled to find Sprague standing beside him.

"That bugger changed course on me. Now he's changed
again, see there? He'll pass clear okay. See there?"

The ensign saw neat clusters of lights on the horizon
now, red and white, green and white, and the ones
Sprague indicated with cigarettefingers, red and green side
by side and white on top but already swinging so that
as they watched the green disappeared.

"Yeah," the ensign said. "My God, he's close."

"It's all right. He's turning, see there? We had him in
the scope all the way in. He scare you?"

"No. In fact I didn't even—"

"You wouldn't mind a little advice, Junior? You should
of been on us for a radar range and C.P.A. long before
this." The ensign did not move, only stood staring back
down at the bow wave. "Why don't you go on down and
get some chow?" Sprague said.

"When my relief gets here."

"That'll be some time. It's Burt Foster, ain't it?"

"I don't know."

"Wait a minute, for God's sake. You was up here when I had the watch five hours ago. You been up here all this time?"

The first time the ensign realized there was a telephone on the bridge was when he saw it in Sprague's hand, ghostly and vague, illuminated solely by the glow when he drew on his cigarette. The light clusters changed patterns and shapes, and the ensign found he was automatically tracking them in his head now just as he had in drills at the Academy. It must have been the bow wave that seduced him. Still, he could not actually, specifically recall the onset of darkness or even describe to himself the sunset.

"Mist' Murphy? This is Sprague. You know you kept this kid up here all this time? Yeah. I don't know anything about Foster or where he's at, but he ain't showed up here. Yeah. Well you better get a relief up here on the double. I think he was asleep—"

"Now just a minute, Sprague, you can't—"

"—but anyway he's done a pretty good job up here and he deserves—oh. Okay."

He may have dozed slightly on his feet, anyway he missed the rest of the conversation. It could only have been a few seconds. Sprague's nose lips eyes hung phantasmagorically in the warm tropic night illuminated by cigaretteglow, then disappeared. Sprague had hold of him, shoving him to the hatch.

The hatch was no longer a black hole, now it was a faint rose, glowing, cool and dry. He was halfway down before he even heard what Sprague had said at the top. "It's okay, Junior. The exec said to go on down. I got the deck."

It gave the ensign an eerie sensation to go through the

upper hatch down into the conning tower then through the lower hatch into the control room (with all the diving gear, the big green diving plane wheels, the blow and vent manifold, the trim manifold, the depth gauges all ominously waiting) and through the heavy watertight door into the forward battery compartment where the wardroom was, as if all those thick hatches stood between him and fresh air and the surface, which of course they did. He wondered if that was how the prisoners felt as the steel doors clanged shut behind them.

The officers had all finished dinner so long ago the table was no longer even set. He washed up, and when he returned to the wardroom the steward was just laying out a paper napkin and upon it setting a bowl of chili, a spoon, and some crackers. The executive officer was sitting at the head of the table in the captain's place, playing acey-deucy with the mustang.

"Mr. Foster," the ensign said. "I believe you were supposed to relieve me."

"Finish this game," the mustang said.

"Steward, I'll skip this course," the ensign said. "Bring on the rest."

But there wasn't any rest. Someone had made a mistake in ordering food and there was only chili. Cans and cans and cans of chili.

"Mistake, hell!" the executive officer snorted. "Somebody made some money off the deal somehow."

"Mr. Murphy, Mr. Foster there was supposed to relieve me but he never showed up."

"I know, I know," the executive officer said. "Just finish this game."

The mustang looked at the ensign and shrugged. "That's what he's been saying all afternoon, kid."

"Mr. Murphy," the ensign said. "I think you should

know that an enlisted man has the watch now. There is no officer on the bridge of this vessel."

"Sprague, you mean? He's had the watch all afternoon in the conning tower."

"Not all afternoon, sir. There was the *steward*—"

"Martinez? Jesus. Be careful. You got to watch him—"

"That's what I—"

"You play acey-deucy?"

"Sir, I have too much work to do. I have some other irregularities to report to you."

"Oh, is that what you are doing? Reporting irregularities?"

"I can't say, sir, that I am truly satisfied, sir, that you—"

"How about liar's dice then?"

"I don't play dice or cards, Mr. Murphy."

"Well, then I'll show you. Really simple enough."

"He's too pure to lie, Murph."

"Oh, I understand the games. I just prefer to devote myself to more elevating things."

The executive officer regarded him silently, then looked back at his game.

"Really, Mr. Murphy, it is close to a disgrace leaving me up there for so long."

"You did okay."

"And Mr. Foster not even caring and then relieving me with an enlisted man."

"Well you see, Junior, we are pretty short-handed. Not everybody made it."

"Missed ship?" the ensign cried. "That's a court-martial offense."

"That a fact, Junior?"

"Mr. Murphy, I have several more irregularities I would like to report."

"Just finish this game first."

"Sir, I must demand to see the captain."

The executive officer rattled the dice.

"He didn't make it either."

The phone whirped. The executive officer had it out of the cradle and to his ear in one motion, studying the acey-deucy board. "What? Okay, Sprague, slow down a little and go under his stern, then get back on course." He looked up at the compass repeater.

"Missed ship?" the ensign cried in outrage. "The captain missed his own ship? Impossible."

"Extenuating circumstances, Admiral. He was taken suddenly drunk." The executive officer pursed his lips and began a tuneless whistle watching the compass repeater while the mustang rolled the dice.

"Mr. Murphy, the way this ship is run is in violation of Naval Regulations and the highest traditions of the service."

"Well, we are sure as hell fortunate to have you here to straighten things out."

"Sir, I intend to make a full report of—"

"Be sure you put in your report that you willfully and persistently interrupted my game of acey-deucy and made playing impossible."

"Sir, I demand to speak to you—"

"All you been doing is speaking to me."

"In private, sir."

The executive officer threw the dice the length of the table, and they rattled off onto the deck. He held his head in his hands.

"Burt, I'll flip you to see who gets to take the watch. There is no place else to hide."

The mustang was already moving out the door, jamming his hat on his head. He wore a tarnished pair of j.g.'s silver bars on his shirt collar, but he still wore his chief's hat. "I always said the wardroom was full of shit. I was better off in the engine room."

The executive officer sat looking at the ensign.

"Sir—"

"Junior, just shut up for a while. Put it all in your report, will you? Can't you find something constructive to do? There honest to God actually is more to being a naval officer than just bitching your head off all the time, I don't care what they told you at the Naval Academy."

The ensign thought a minute.

"I'll work out some plans."

"For what?"

"Rules and regulations for leaving ship in a foreign port, the fair and equitable establishment of duty section rosters and related items. Conduct ashore. Personal hygiene, if you uh know what I mean—"

"I'm afraid I do."

"—without careful planning and organization the men just don't know what to do in a liberty port and it hurts the morale. I'll find out about museums, churches, cultural events. I may give some language lessons myself. I speak Spanish *muy bueno*. I'll promulgate some orders on this if I may, sir."

"You go ahead and promulgate, Junior. Do you good."

A sailor appeared in the doorway with two shotguns and a six-pack of beer. "If you don't have anything better to do," he said, "I thought we might work on these, get 'em oiled up. I broke this out of the cold box aft."

The executive officer made a gesture of welcome, and the sailor came right on into the wardroom, jostling the ensign a little, and put the shotguns down on the wardroom table along with the beer and produced a beercanopener from among the huge cluster of keys he wore at his belt. He opened the beer—

"Junior?"

"No thank you."

—and in companionable silence the two men began dissembling the shotguns. Martinez appeared with a platter of crackers and yellow cheese. A chief petty officer wearing a dress blue uniform with red hashmarks up to the elbow and a shiny new hat came in with another chief who wore only a chief's hat and dungarees and carried a Thompson submachine gun. They sat talking and drinking and working, laughing and smoking, and somebody came with more beer and a platter of cold cuts from the crew's mess aft, and the P.A. system was playing jazzy records.

As the ensign made his way along the passageway, Sprague approached, carrying a bottle of rum, which he held up. "This against regulations, Junior?"

"Absolutely. There is no liquor allowed in vessels of the United—"

"Good. Good for you. Just testing you." He moved on by.

"Sprague—in the wardroom there. There is a chief in his dress blue uniform. I didn't know anybody aboard even owned one, let alone wore it."

"Chekenian you mean? Been in the Navy forty-two years and he just made chief last month. Wants to get his money's worth out of the suit. Little snort? Just the thing when you get off watch. In fact, with Foster up there we'll probably all need it. He's a chief engineman, you know."

"Mr. Foster is an officer."

"That's what you and him and the Navy thinks. But he's just an engineman."

Sprague went on into the wardroom, and the ensign wandered off aft.

About an hour later the group in the wardroom was interrupted by the hum of the 1 m.c. and a familiar high-pitched voice shouting, "Now hear this! Now hear this! This is the assistant navigator speaking. All hands will assemble in the *bloop—*"

Sprague had the phone out of the cradle at once, calling the control room. When he hung up, he said,

"It was the kid. He told the chief he had a short announcement but it turned out he wanted to assemble all hands at quarters in the crew's mess right now. So he cut him off."

"Maybe he will turn in now," the executive officer said. "He must be very tired."

"When he gets shook down he might be okay."

"Jackie tell you where she'd be staying?"

"No. I was asleep when she left. I figured she'd tell you."

"Yeah. I heard about that. Well, you ought to turn in yourself."

"With Foster up there?"

"Yeah. Well. Who do we have to relieve him?"

"The ensign."

"That bad, huh?"

"Like you said, it's only ninety miles."

"Yeah. Okay. I'm going to catch a little shuteye."

"I'll call you when we pick up the pilot."

"Hell. I forgot about him."

"The ensign won't."

4

The pilot came out to meet the submarine just after midnight in a small motor launch with a bright white light. He had trouble getting aboard, but Sprague and another sailor got down on their knees and boosted him up over the tank tops and brought him up to the bridge.

"*Gracias, señores.*"

"Jesus," Sprague said. "Don't you speak any English at all?"

"*Por seguro, señor*. Heet eez vair dark *esta noche*, no?"

"Oh no," Sprague said. "Not again."

"Tell him to get his ass off and go on back," the executive officer said.

"No!" the ensign said. He had changed into a dress gabardine khaki uniform for entering port and seemed to glow with a radiance all his own on the dark bridge. "We can't do that. Mr. Batista might be offended."

"Screw Batista."

"*Shhhh!* Officers and men of the United States Navy on foreign soil are emissaries of the United States government. We have to be diplomats without portfolio."

"Tell him in diplomatic language we don't have any use for a pilot that can't speak English and to get his ass off and go tell Batista to—"

"No!" the ensign said. "Naval Regulations require the

presence of a qualified pilot whenever a vessel enters a foreign port."

"This isn't a foreign port, for Christ's sake," Sprague said. "This is Havana."

"Naval Regulations specifically require—"

"All right," the executive officer said. "You talk to him. Ask him about the wind and the current and which way to go to get in the damn entrance channel."

"*Como?*" the ensign said. "No. Wait. Uh. *Quanto es*— no. *Esta. Quanto esta* uh—"

The pilot began to speak rapidly in Spanish, waving his arms the whites of his eyes flashing in the dark.

"Ask him what he means," the executive officer said. "Go on. Hurry up."

"*Que* uh—" the ensign said. "No. Wait. Uhhh *que esta usted* uh no wait. Lemmesee. Uh. *Comment allez-vous*—"

"That's French, for God's sake."

"I always found French quite simple, even though many of my classmates had considerable difficulty with it. Actually all languages are pretty easy when you put your mind to them. It's all in listening and understanding the psychology of the people. I intend to give lessons to the crew as soon as—"

"All ahead one third," the executive officer said. His cigarette glowed in the dark as he waved toward the bow. "Steer that way."

Sprague shouted down the hatch for some periscope bearings, then called a course to the helm as they picked up steerageway.

"*Tiene usted una* Chesterfield?" the pilot said.

"What?" the ensign said.

"He wants a cigarette," Sprague said, giving him one. The pilot subsided, smoking, watching the water rush by.

When they tied up finally to a long pier with a big

warehouse on it the ensign said, "That wasn't bad. You must have done this before."

"About one thousand fucking times," Sprague said.

"But we've never done it before with such class," the executive officer said. "With our own translator and everything."

"*Ustedes quieres mujeres?*" the pilot said.

"What?" the ensign said.

"He wants to know if you want some women," Sprague said.

"Why would he say a thing like that?" the ensign said.

"He doubles as one of Batista's cultural representatives," the executive officer said.

"What did he say just then?" the ensign said.

"He said his sister is a virgin with big tits and hot pants," Sprague said. "And for ten bucks he'll introduce you."

"That's terrible," the ensign said.

"You said it. Used to be two bucks."

"It's Batista," the executive officer said. "He's getting the other eight dollars. Put that in your report, Junior."

"There is a man down there leaving the ship!" the ensign said. "Stop him!"

"What for?" Sprague said.

"I have prepared a duty roster," the ensign said.

"A what?" the executive officer said from beneath the turtleback. He had one foot down the hatch.

"I inquired for one and was told one could not be found. So I prepared one. Regulations require that we keep one third of the crew aboard while we are in port. Here is the list of those who may go on liberty. This insures that the ship is in compliance with Regulations and is ready for sea at all times."

"Kid, we are lucky if we had much more than a third

of the crew aboard when we left Key West. If we keep a third aboard there won't be anybody in the liberty party."

The ensign held his flashlight against the paper in his hand. "Nonetheless, sir, we must adhere to established naval procedures and—"

"Okay, Junior," the executive officer said halfway down the hatch. "Suit yourself."

"Aye, aye, sir," the ensign said, juggling his flashlight and paper to snap off a perfect salute. "I'll hold inspection, then declare liberty for those in the liberty section after breakfast. If they pass inspection, of course."

The ensign stood alone on the bridge in the tropic night holding his flashlight to his paper. Somebody got a gangway light rigged and now the ensign could see a steady stream of sailors, some in dirty whites, some in blues, some still in greasy dungarees, flowing over the brow and gathering in groups on the pier. Taxicabs were appearing and in their headlightglow girls stood talking to the sailors. Some paired off and got into the cabs and some disappeared into the warehouse.

Sprague appeared, a bottle in his hand, running across the brow waving at a cab.

The ensign shouted, a thin high sound in the sultry night laced now with raucous Cuban music from the cars. The only one who heard him was a sailor just coming along the deck at the base of the conning tower.

"What?" the sailor said. "You want what?"

"The executive officer! Please ask him to come up here immediately!"

The sailor pointed forward toward the forward torpedo room hatch. The executive officer was just stepping out in his neat uniform of wash khaki.

"Mr. Murphy!" the ensign cried. "You're supposed to wear a blouse ashore!"

The executive officer did not pause or even really acknowledge beyond a wave the ensign's voice.

"*Mr. Murphy!—*"

"What?" shielding his eyes against the moonlight as he looked up. "What is it?"

"The crew—duty section—they aren't even—"

"*What?*"

"Sprague! Look there—he—"

"Oh! Thanks. See him." He walked on over and got into the cab, Sprague holding the door open and yelling at the driver, and then they were driving off.

Again the ensign shouted in that thin and reedy voice which seemed as far as the crew was concerned to blend with the exuberant nightsounds which could now be seen rounding the far corner of the warehouse: a roving Cuban band of some sort: young men and women dancing or anyway writhing and singing or anyway shouting and pounding on strange instruments. Some wore frilled white blouses and fancy headgear. Some did not seem to be wearing much at all. There were lots of women.

"Get away from here!" the ensign cried. "Go away!" But he could barely hear himself shout. He ran down and over the brow and onto the pier. The pier seemed to undulate beneath his feet and the Cuban women were everywhere, surprisingly clean-looking and pretty. The air smelled of their perfume and there was something lascivious about the tropical night itself.

"You just breathe," a sailor said, breathing deeply, "and you get a hard on."

The sailor threw his arm around a girl and walked off. The ensign ran back aboard the submarine. The moon-struck decks seemed covered with chalk, a phantom ship in a phantom sea, beautiful beyond thought. He was breathing hard and he found it outrageous that what the sailor said was true.

He made his way across the deck, ignoring as best he could the movement and noise of the party on the pier. He went down the forward torpedo room hatch and then through the submarine, trying to find out which sailors were going ashore and which were staying.

"You in the duty or the liberty section?" he would say.

"Don't know."

"You don't *know?*" the ensign screamed. "You can't run a ship this way."

"This ain't a ship anyway," the sailor said, pulling on his white jumper. "It's a submarine."

"Where is the duty officer?" the ensign cried, his voice so shrill and young it got tangled in the submarine's endless machinerynoise and lost. "I demand to see the duty officer."

In that class of submarine the officers' head was in the after starboard corner of the forward torpedo room, just forward of the watertight door to the battery compartment. As the ensign was ducking through the door, stepping over the coaming, a loud and singular sound announced itself through the thin metal door of the head.

"You can hear him anyway, Mr. Hillerby."

"What?" the ensign said, bumping his head.

"He's in there, Mr. Foster is."

"No. He had the duty in Key West."

"Well he lost the acey-deucy game so he's got it here too."

Through the door the mustang's tenor came: "What is it? What's all the fuss?" over the comfortable domestic sound of the toiletpaper roll being batted.

"I'm looking for the duty officer."

"Well?"

The ensign stood staring at the metal door in helpless outrage trying to find the proper attitude, fighting off the image of the mustang's hygienic posture and undignified attitude. They had not taught him at the Naval Academy to deal with that. More sounds came through the door. The ensign began to shout. "I am Ensign Hillerby! I—"

"Awright awright, for gawdsake, can't you even let a man take a—"

"—request permission to go ashore!"

"What? Say that again. You what?"

In the diesel and sweatsmelling torpedo room the breathing of not only the ensign but of the invisible mustang too was audible as all the sailors stood frozen in various extravagant attitudes craning around toward where the ensign stood at a Naval Academy inspection brace heels together thumbs along the once immaculate now oil- and greasestained trousers, necktie awry, hat visor over one ear, staring straight ahead at the metal door behind which the mustang crouched at his invisible but audible task.

"Ensign Hillerby, sir. I request permission to leave the ship and go ashore."

"For God's sake, Hillerby, this is Havana."

At the forward end of the room the great torpedo tubes stood, serene cylinders deadly and poised, and all around the room the giant torpedoes were stored. This had for the short time he had been aboard given the ensign a sinking and eerie feeling in his stomach each time he walked through, because the submarine itself was a deadly weapon and this was the muzzle where he stood among the bullets requiring only some idiot's finger on the trigger somewhere to shoot everything including him out through the tubes into the black and endless water. It did not seem to bother the sailors any, some of whom slept so intimately with the torpedoes they turned in the night and embraced them giving rise to all manner of obscene and sailorly conjecture about the look and proper classification of the issue of such a union should the sailor manage finally to fulfill the absolute and inviolable law of seamen to screw anything that would hold still long enough.

"What?" the ensign shouted over machinerynoise and the whoosh of the airblowers. "What's that supposed to—"

"He means you can go ashore, Mist' Hillerby," a sailor said just behind him, standing naked at the washbasin, his lathered face twisted around, razor poised, dripping, loins twisted semidistended organ visible. *Why they are animals*, the ensign thought. *Just animals.*

"Yes, all right," the ensign shouted. "I am going ashore, sir. When is liberty up?"

"When everybody is back aboard!" the mustang said. "Now go away and leave me alone. I got a right to my privacy too."

The ensign actually saluted then, so fiercely and inaccurately he struck the side of his canted visor and spun the immaculate hat up over his head and onto the greasy deck. The naked sailor tried to grab it before it landed, lurched against the ensign, then leaned to the deck retrieving, presenting a hairy backside to the ensign's appalled view.

"You're out of uniform!" the ensign cried.

"Here's your hat, sir," the sailor said, resuming with his other hand his shave which made a sandpaper sound.

"Yes! Thank you! We'll see about all this!"

He clamped his hat on his head and marched stumbling off in dignity, not neglecting in his haste to bump his head again against the low top in stepping through the watertight door.

When he reached the pier he found a taxicab, an ancient unrecognizable car with no top, not a convertible, a sedan of some kind, survivor of some total disaster, the doors all welded shut to hold the body together. He climbed in shouting at the driver and the cab pulled off while he was still hopping along on one foot.

The ensign sat in fierce immobility, the stained hat jammed down around his ears from where he had bumped his head, staring straight ahead not through the windshield because there was none the perfumed wind tugging and pulling at his face like a woman's hand.

In the steady cascade of Spanish from the front seat the ensign realized he had been hearing for some time now a repeated phrase he could actually understand.

"You want to go weeth ozzair offeesairs?"

He took the driver under fire with careful phrasebook Spanish, but all he got back was the reiterated phrase, so he said, "All right, all right, *si señor si señor,*" realizing as he said it it made no difference. He was going where the driver assumed he would go.

5

He was delivered to a dingy building on the waterfront with the name *Bahia* in decayed and sputtering neon. Not far away was a yacht basin, masts and cabintops silhouetted against the moonstruck bay. He thought he had been duped, swindled by a foreign devil and was already shouting at the retreating taxicab as he tried the door and found himself tumbled into what appeared to be a setting from an old Carmen Miranda movie with ravenhaired women dancing and the smoke and the fiery Latin music and tables jammed together on the small and crowded floor and somebody was calling his name.

"Hillerby! Hillerby! Over here!"

It was a group of men from the submarine forming a kind of island in the sea of bodies and tables, a bunch of the little tables pushed together all grouped together like that in their uniforms and hats. The hats outraged him as holding his own carefully and respectfully in his hand he made his way over until he realized the hats were not on the men but on the women.

One of the women was wearing not only a hat but a naval officer's blouse of tan gabardine with the black and gold shoulder boards of a lieutenant commander. He noticed her particularly because she came toward him and attempted to embrace him. She had nothing on beneath the blouse. Laughter grew and reverberated and hands were touching him pulling him and he was seated a drink in his hand guarding carefully his hat on the table before him staring at it in amazement. How had it got so dirty?

The girl in the officer's blouse and hat was going up the stairs with Sprague and the ensign wondered if he would have her keep them on while he—*thus screwing symbolically the officercorps,* the ensign thought wildly. *He can't—*

"Hillerby, have you met my wife?"

Frozen in the crowded, smoky room, he found himself staring into the calm eyes which seemed to contain here even more than before a question of great consequence which he could not quite comprehend.

"Well, she won't bite you, for God's sake, sit still."

It was a voice he had never heard though he had since reading his orders to the submarine had dreams and nightmares about how it might sound and now would never forget: the captain, his commanding officer, surprisingly not even a full commander (the ensign thought though did not know he thought thus could not deny that he felt any officer in command of any ship *he* served in should be at least an admiral) but a fat lieutenant commander the rank announced solely by the small gold oak leaves on the sweatcurled collarpoints: the captain smoking a thin cigar, lounging back in the cheap wooden chair that had borne the assaults of uncounted thousands of naval tourists seeking God only knew what from the smoke and music and foreign flesh, bereft of hat tie blouse and now the ensign realized the girl upstairs with Sprague had been (was possibly even now, still, while—) wearing his blouse.

"Don't tell me you've forgotten me already?"

Her low voice burrowed easily through the noise and he worried that she would mention just yesterday on the submarine how would he explain that protect her honor but she was already quite casually describing their meeting. Her pale blond hair was all soft highlights, neatly combed.

"From the looks of him he needs a good steak dinner and a few hours upstairs. Huh, kid? Right?" The captain interrupted himself with laughter which grew and fed upon itself, obliterating conversation, and anyway some sort of floorshow had begun with the shouting of the singers and the leaping and jerking of the dancers and the incredible instrumental cacophony the ensign's classically trained ear refused to accept as music.

For the first time since his arrival he was not the center of attention and he could take muster, prepare his case of dereliction and general incompetence for the court-martial proceedings he would personally—

"Buy me a dreenk, honey, okay?"

It was one of the women who went with the place insinuated with an abrupt deft motion in his lap, bare breasts angling toward his face and when he tried to turn her away he found himself looking just across the loose and now (she was laughing) faintly jiggling breasts into Jacqueline's somber eyes though only the eyes were somber: she was laughing too. She did not move only sat smoking and laughing with the others, regarding him with that curious intensity as if trying to recall some terrible moment in her life with which he might have been or might have yet to be concerned.

She was wearing a lightyellow dress and there was about her in the midst of the frantic gaiety the same aura of air-conditioned cool she had displayed yesterday. As he returned her gaze across the animated breasts he noticed a cigarette come to her lips, but it was a man's hand in a khaki sleeve that held it. Then the ensign realized that beside her sat the executive officer immaculate starched and icycool, regarding him with that familiar look opaque and private. It could have been disdain.

"Well, Junior," he said, but then all sound was obliterated as the woman turned abruptly toward him and embraced him, pulling his head to her breasts. He struggled slightly, then sank in sweet warmth incredible softness all sound muffled by her bosom. Later he became aware that Jacqueline was no longer there.

Everybody was dancing. The music (*That isn't music*, the ensign thought, *that's just caterwauling*) and the shouting and whooping and yipping the ensign supposed was singing were all mixed up with the smoke and the whirling bodies and the glimpses of—wait. That girl out there in the middle of the jampacked floor was abso*lute*ly naked, but the crowd closed around her, them, and the girl on his lap was wriggling and squirming and kind of keeping time with the music or something right on his lap and her legs and his hand and her breasts and the first thing he knew his hand was actually—*hey, Junior!*

"What?"

"Yer daddy wants yuh."

"Listen, damn it, I'm—"

"I can see that, but I won't tell. Go see yer daddy." It was a sailor, just a grin hanging in the dim thick air.

The ensign felt like a man in one of those slow-motion sequences in the movies everything velvet warm cottony unreal the disembodied grin repeating the message until finally it was the girl who ceased, changed, was no longer there, moving from the ensign to the sailor, a universe in a single soft bound.

Then the ensign saw the executive officer looking not at him but at the stairs and on the stairs Jacqueline and the fat lieutenant commander. She seemed to be struggling.

"Look!" the ensign cried. "Look at that!"

The executive officer turned. "Oh, Junior, they tell you? Your dad's outside."

"Honest?" No: she wasn't struggling. She was hurrying.

"Cross my heart," doing so with the suave cool fingers that held the burning cigarette, handsome face impassive.

The ensign threw himself furiously through the crowd, emerging finally by the stairway, running up two, three at a time. He reached them several paces down the hallway, just at the threshold of a room with a pink door.

"—but a whore's room—" the commanding officer was saying.

"Well why not?" she said. The perfumed voice had kind of a hard lacquer finish now, he would not have recognized it, or the eyes, or the face for that matter. "What's the difference now?"

"Difference? My God, you've—"

"You want another woman too? You want to send for—look who's here!"

The captain turned and saw the ensign. All sound disappeared. They regarded each other in absolute silence immobile and guarded. The ensign was the first to move. He saluted. "Ensign Hillerby reporting for duty, sir. I—I mean I haven't actually met, uh, introduced—"

The captain looked at Jacqueline. "What? Who—oh no, now wait, that's too much, I won't—"

"No, no, I didn't send for him, know he was coming did I, hon—what is it they call him—Junior?"

They stood informed by the same fantastic thought, and then it vanished and probably none but the ensign would ever think it again and then only in bits and snatches which he would immediately deny even to himself.

Her eyes caught his in the mirror. "What's a nice kid

like you doing in a place like this?" she said. She had a low, crooning laugh. Her hair was disheveled now.

They were standing together in the open doorway of the stark room furnished with a bed and little else save a profusion of cheap mirrors in one of which the ensign saw the sight which would haunt him for the rest of his life: the three of them inside the room just by the bed Jacqueline and the captain arm in arm and his head between theirs.

"Well, Junior—" the captain said.

"So now you're doing it too."

"Doing what?"

"Calling me Junior."

The captain only looked at him.

"He doesn't even know my name," the ensign said.

"Come on," Jacqueline said. She said it to the captain, not the ensign. She was still looking in the mirror tugging on the captain's arm. Looking over their shoulders the ensign saw on her face an expression ancient fierce and wanton, peculiarly increased by the prim cut of the light-yellow dress. Then he noticed, craning to look closely at her where she stood so close he could smell her, the pointy nipple bump just there though of course it could have been his imagination. It was after all his imagination that knew the shape and feel of her breasts. She was deep-chested and breathing hard, her nostrils tender crisp bud-like flaring.

They stood poised on the threshold of something just beyond reach or even thought. Her arm worked around the captain's barrellike middle and the ensign saw in the way the graceful fingers grasped the khaki shirt a world within a world distant contained impregnable *listen:* behind them the hustle and bustle of continuous traffic in the passageway girls going this way and that with sailors officers and even an occasional civilian (when he learned later that some of the men were actually the girls' husbands come to see they were on the job he refused to believe it *why they are just animals* he thought) the girls quiet and grim up here (no laughingdancingsinging) hurrying right along businesslike purposeful severe looking tired and much older than they had downstairs. They entered the rooms in pairs, a girl and a man, but left one at a time, looking strangely sad as if the only real gaiety was downstairs after all.

Then the ensign turned his image flickering from the mirror in which they stared transfixed and grabbed one of the passing girls hustling her fiercely toward the first open door down the hallway. She was not all that eager, struggling tiredly, which only excited him.

"No, no," she said. "I got to get the hokay—you can't just—"

"Never mind that." He hustled her in and shut the door. It was an identical stark room, the cheap swayback bed repository of the fantasies of probably the entire U.S. fleet, the inferior mirrors everywhere, some so bad there was a touch of the funhouse in the wavering eccentric reflections. Which was the only place he looked, the mirrors; he had not really even seen the girl yet, only her reflection standing beside him, their images gravely undulating at the slightest movement. He spoke to her reflections as if she were across the room.

"Get undressed now."

"No I tole you I got to get the hokay from—"

"Here! See? All for you! Now get undressed, and remember, your name is Jacqueline."

The show of money calmed her. She palmed the bills in some extraordinary way, neither putting them in her clothing anywhere because that would all come off now nor placing them in the room because it was no more her room than it was his, then took off all her clothes while he watched her in the mirror.

It was not the wildly sensual scene he had imagined. One or two quick motions and she stood nude uncoy uncaring and frank, arms hanging like a woman stripped for a physical examination, her only expression a look of patient suffering as if the complaint that had brought her to the clinic was chronic and severe.

"I yam Yackalon," she said, cool and unquestioning. It was not the oddest thing she had ever been asked to do. "Ho boy honney yew got me all hexcited what you wanna do now." She put her thumbs beneath her arms in the manner of an old man strutting and it took him a while to understand she was thus elevating her shopworn breasts.

"You just want *me*, don't you Jackie?"

"*Si. Usted.* Honly *usted.*"

"None of those others, certainly not that fat—"

"Look, babee, I ain't got this much time."

Driven by time and a polished business sense—she had the money now and the only thing between her and more was him standing there yakking—she went to the bed, the multiple rippling images converging where she presented herself in an attitude so pornographic he was actually shocked.

"Wait!" he said. "Wait—don't—"

"Come on babee you got Yackalon so hot she doan know what to do come on what you got for Yackalon huh queek—"

"Wait. Actually, what I had in mind was more that you should—"

Three or four sharp loud raps sounded at the door and by the time the last one sounded she had her clothes on.

She moved so quickly she was fully dressed before he realized the incredible place she had secreted the money.

"Wait—" he said. "That isn't sanitary."

But she was already opening the door. *Well,* he thought. *Anyway it's appropriate.*

In the doorway stood a sailor, his arm around a girl. "This is the green door, right? We got this room. What the hell's the big—"

"*Nada nada* jus a meestake. Scuse—" she said slipping neatly by the sailor and down the hallway, leaving the ensign standing in the room squaring away his hat, his tie. He worked his way by the big sailor, drawing himself up, full military bearing then to his own horror saw himself saluting in all the mirrors grave little boy in the funhouse something like a full battalion passing in review drunkenly leaving behind the closing door the sailor watching the girl who was already stripping, chewing gum. *Thank God he's not from my ship: he didn't call me Junior.*

He walked down the hall but not very far. At the pink door he paused, hating himself, trying to listen. Nothing. Just as he was going on a huge darkskinned Cuban man came down the hall, a really handsome specimen with his onyx hair and small fine features and muscles bulging through his open shirt and white pants so tight they were obscene.

"No," the ensign said. "Not the pink door. That room is taken."

The Cuban man only flashed him a brilliant grin though around the eyes was the same hollow preoccupation the girls' eyes showed, knocked softly, and entered before receiving a reply. The ensign's eyes ached but found only walls and empty mirrors—wait. Just as the door closed he had a glimpse tantalizing and incomplete which for years his brain would try to fathom and then forget.

Dazed, he descended the stairs, realizing halfway down he had superseded the floorshow as the main attraction, everybody watching him, yelling things. They were running up to meet him, almost like a race. Sprague won.

Roughhandling him, shouting in his ear, Sprague muscled him through the jampacked room and through the door at the other side, shouting, "There! There! How many times you got to be told? Yer daddy wants ya! Now get outa here so we can have a good time!"

6

The door closed behind him. The ensign stood in moonlight, touching his necktie, squaring his filthy hat, feeling for his wallet which somehow had gone. Then he remembered he had left it in his blouse which he had left in the room.

He saw the car, dark and furtive, a cigarette glowing through the windshield.

"Now look!" he cried. "You promised. You said you wouldn't—"

"I didn't," the admiral's voice said, disembodied but strong. The engine coughed to life and the lights snapped on. Across the admiral's head and shoulders outlined in dashglow the ensign saw there was somebody sitting beside him, smallish, indubitably feminine.

"Mary Beth!"

"Jimmie, where on earth *were* you? What were you *doing* all this time? We've been *waiting* out here the *longest* time—"

"Get in, son."

The admiral had the car moving smoothly through the soft Havana night. The yacht basin retreated, the masts black lines against the moonstruck sky. Beside him the ensign was aware of Mary Beth's familiar floral perfume, sweet and wholesome. Through the open window Havana's earthy fragrance beckoned. He rolled the window up.

"Admiral, you said after graduation my career was my own to worry about. I thought you meant that."

"Of course I did."

"Then what are you doing down here? You going to tell me it was just a coincidence?"

"No, no, Mary Beth here called me. Right after you'd called her with the news you were going to the *Devilfish*. I happened to be with the captain of the *Devilfish* when I got the news. I had to have him flown here to catch his ship, so I decided I might as well make an excursion out of it so I invited his wife and Mary Beth to come along."

"And yourself."

"Jimmie, you might have told me about this diesel foolishness. My God, son, you are all lined up for nuclear school. You've got to get right back if you expect to—"

"Admiral—" Mary Beth said. "We agreed not to go into that right away. We'll work it out."

"Go into what?" the ensign said.

"You going to show me Havana?" Mary Beth said. "I'd just adore to see Havana by moonlight."

"It's pretty late."

"Of course he'll show you Havana by moonlight, Mary Beth. No question about it. Tell you how we'll work this, Jimmie. We'll just drop back by the hotel where you and I can have a drink and Mary Beth can freshen up and then you can show her the city. Okay?"

"I don't really want a drink, sir."

"Course you do. Want to hear about your trip over."

Mary Beth went up to her room. The admiral and the ensign sat in the bar of the Nacional Hotel.

"Well, that's very interesting, son. Quite a cruise. So

she is undermanned and poorly run. Glad you understand that, observed that."

"That's not the half of it. There was a little game of chicken of the sea that—"

"Of what?" The admiral bottomed his whiskey and set it down.

"Chicken of the—"

"Care for another Coca-Cola, Jimmie?"

"No, thank you, sir. The executive officer called it chicken of the sea. He saw this other submarine coming—"

"We'll have a little coffee in my room."

"No, thank you, sir. I've got to be getting back to the submarine."

But the admiral was up and moving across the bar of the Nacional, a large man in a neat seersucker suit, looking to the ensign peculiarly naked, indecent without his blue serge uniform with its thick bands of gold lace, sailors and officers saluting on every side.

He passed beneath the downfunneled light from a ceiling fixture, and the ensign was struck by how vulnerable the head looked, fragile and exposed without the heavy armor of the admiral's hat, protected solely by the thin and somehow childlike gray hair. It grew in a thinning whorl at the crown.

Besides the toilet gear laid out as neatly as surgical instruments on a folded towel in the bathroom, the single personal item visible in the admiral's hotel room was the electric coffeepot, his constant traveling companion.

The admiral, preoccupied, had with automatic frugality snapped on only one lamp, the small one nearest the coffeepot. They sat in semidarkness, the terrace doors open, Havana lurking outside. The night was softening beyond redemption, already laced with the cool smell of morning, and now the aroma of freshbrewed coffee.

"Believe I'll have some of that after all, sir."

"Ready in a minute. Soon as the little light comes on."

That's regulation, the ensign thought. *To wait for the light. He wouldn't violate the instructions and pour half a minute early. He wouldn't know how.*

"Now, Jimmie, we really have to talk about nuclear-power school. The *Devilfish* is—well, it has a bad reputation. You've seen why. You'll damage your career. You don't want the *Devilfish* in your record—"

"The *Devilfish* is a disgrace to the Navy," the ensign said. "I don't understand how they have hung on this long, how they can exist another day. All they think about is—wait. I've got all their names right here—my notebook—"

He put his hand in one pocket then the other then stood frantically slapping his trousers fore and aft, then his shirt and back to his trousers. "Well goddam son of a bitch!"

"What?"

"I must have left that in my blouse too!"

"I've never heard you swear before."

"That little bitch!"

"What have they done to my only son?"

The admiral's voice had a funny tone the ensign had never heard before. Or anyway noticed. Because just there with his hands for perhaps the seventh or eighth time making their futile tour of his empty pockets the ensign was struck by the realization that he had heard the tone before but never let himself admit it. Was it possible the admiral had after all a subtle sense of humor? No, it was not possible and he renewed his assault on his pockets until the admiral told him for God's sake to sit down.

"But it's all in there. Their names—"

"I know their names—"

"—and what they do. The things they've done."

"I know most of that too."

"Then you are already investigating."

The admiral pulled at his coffeecup, his lips pursed. "In a manner of speaking you might say that, yes." Again there was the voicetone. In the dimness the ensign could not see the admiral's eyes. He was looking now away from him, out the open terrace doors.

"It can't be allowed!" the ensign cried. "We have to straighten them out. The whole damn ship. Bring them back into the U. S. Navy. Teach them to run a taut ship. The things they do. I—I've got a list here. Had. In my notebook. When the police find—never mind. I can remember most of it."

"I'm sure you can. You know, Jimmie, maybe you—"

"And their personal life. Their morals. Their—my God you simply couldn't believe—"

"You mean Jacqueline, I suppose."

"Then you know—"

"I know she is an extraordinarily attractive young lady—"

"*Lady?* My God, she is immoral as an alley cat."

"She speaks very highly of you."

"I'm sure I couldn't care less what a woman like that says about me. What did she say?"

"She said she thought you were a real gentleman, a breath of fresh air. A good example for the others."

"Example? They wouldn't know a good example if they —bah! They're not worth talking about. We shouldn't be wasting our time on them. It's demeaning. Just have them all court-martialed. They can't get that ship out of the harbor without pulling enough stuff to keep a dozen courts-martial busy for years. Not only the so-called officers. There's an enlisted man named Sprague who—"

"He's her lover too."

"He what?"

"Used to be, anyway. So they say. Somewhere along the line. Retired now, you might say, from active duty. That's why he's in the crew."

"You mean the—her—Feldman and Murphy—they don't know?"

The admiral shrugged. "It isn't much of a secret. They aren't like other people, Jimmie. They have their own rules."

"But my God she—they wouldn't just—"

"She still likes him. Or feels responsible, anyway maintains her interest and affection—"

"My God, she carries her past along with her like—"

"We all do, don't we Jimmie? In one form or another. She's just different about it. But then she's different about a lot of things. I mean, we'd all respect her more if she'd cut him dead and pretend she never knew him, right? Because we're moral. But she does things her own way."

The ensign stared at the admiral's face which now, because of the way he had turned, had a certain moonlike aspect, half in darkness the other half soft and vague. Beside him the red light on the coffeepot glowed steady and hard.

"We shouldn't even be thinking about those people, let alone talking about them. It's a waste of time. They're just scum. I don't want to say one more word about them. Which one of those guys is she really married to anyway?"

The admiral turned slowly, the moon revolving. There was a small contained explosion of light in his face, then another red hole rent the darkness, this one moving, tracing the path of the admiral's hand as he gestured.

"Jacqueline isn't really married to either of them. Al-

though she is the what do they call it when you—when you
live together—"

"Shack up."

"—for a long time. No, no. It's—"

"Mistress."

"Well, that's the glamorous term, I suppose, but it
doesn't have any legal status, and that's what she wanted.
Because she actually tried to have herself declared his—"

The lightsoft features glowed red, illumined from below
as he pulled on the cigarette.

"Commonplace wife—" the ensign cried, the thin reedy
voice querulous, as if his own honor were being somehow
impugned.

"No, yes, that's it. Common-law wife."

"She can't do that, get away with that."

"I never could figure out if she did. It may all very—"

"Regulations wouldn't allow it."

"There's nothing in Naval Regulations about it. It's apparently the one thing Naval Regulations overlooked. Cus-
tom and tradition is where you find all that. But Congress
never passed those."

"Anyway if it was just *living with*—she'd be both their
what you said. Common-law wives. Wouldn't she?"

"She never could make up her mind. That was always a
weakness with her."

"She didn't seem to me to have any more weaknesses
than an iron nail might, or maybe a knife or a marlin-
spike."

"She was engaged to Orin Feldman at the Naval Academy."

"Now you're going to tell me she went to the Naval
Academy—"

"She might have, knowing Jackie, if she'd really wanted
to. But no, she was in love with Orin, probably would have

ended up a matronly Navy wife expert on children and moving she's always had that crazy streak of practicality. Or romance, or whatever."

"So what happened?"

"She and Orin were discovered in *flagrante delicto* as the report put it, in Orin's bunk in Bancroft Hall—"

"At the Academy! Holy cow! How did—"

"By Harold."

"Harold?"

"Murphy. Your exec. Handsome Harold they called him then. Called him in the yearbook. Guess they still do. He had the security watch that night."

"Aha! So Feldman—" the ensign could not bring himself to call him captain now "was bilged out of the Academy."

"No. Murphy didn't report it."

"Why not?"

"Why else? Jacqueline."

"What could she do about it?"

The admiral's chin and nose glowed red. His eyes were dark mooncraters. "Are you serious, Jimmie? Are you really asking me that?"

The ensign watched the cigarettend trace its arc through the dimness. He heard the gentle coffeesplash, the clinkclank of the spoon and he realized he had always found that spoon noise troubling, inconsistent with the admiral's absolute and unremitting consistency: he always took his coffee black and bitter, regulation Navystyle: but he always stirred it.

"She really did that? Did it? There? Right there?"

"So the story goes."

"With *Murphy?*"

"Look, Jimmie, if you—"

"No. Wait. Feldman. How about him? You mean he *allowed* it?"

"He didn't have much choice did he? If he wanted to stay in the Academy. Which of course he did. And out of jail. Jacqueline was in high school then. What's the term? Jailbait."

The morning sky had brightened. The final star had gone. The ensign could see the admiral's face more clearly from the reflected morninglight, could see the heavy Academy class ring on the hand that held the cup. The ensign held his coffeecup in his left hand too, a habit that coincided with the purchase of his own ornate and heavy class ring, like his father's, and had as well now a tendency to elevate the fifth and fourth fingers as he drank, to flash the ring.

"But that's terrible!" the ensign cried.

"Probably."

"Well, how about Feldman. He got—you know."

"It's okay, Jimmie. You can say it. Nobody here but us and I'll never tell. Fucked. Well, people who know the story, maybe it's a legend now, conjecture a lot about that. That debate has warmed many a cold gray wardroom on the high seas. Had Feldman got his before—"

"Did he just stand there and watch?"

"Depends on which version you hear. You'll have to ask him yourself someday. Or her." The admiral allowed himself a faint smile.

"So she left Feldman for Murphy."

"If she'd left him, thrown him over clean, he would have gotten over it in time. Found some nice frowsy gal to keep house and have fat babies and move every two years and wear a miniature class ring and work her ass off to have nice dinner parties for all the right senior officers. He'd have made admiral for sure. Some say CNO. But she couldn't leave Orin alone. Handsome Harold bored her. So she went back to Orin Feldman."

"He should have—"

"Should have? A terrible phrase, Jimmie. They should all have done a lot of things differently. Maybe even they realize that now. But they were young and Jackie was, well, Jackie, and you know, I imagine, how the boys at the Academy are even today, way they treat them like monks, their balls aching all the time. Feldman was glad enough to get her back but then Harold Murphy couldn't leave her alone either and they finally worked out their whatever you call it. Their arrangement. Understanding."

7

The admiral was taking shape now in the steadily brightening room, the body sketching in rapidly beneath the ghostly hand: the neat seersucker suit, the regulation white shirt and plain black navy tie, the polished monkstrap shoes of regulation black calf. The remnants of the night lay only in the dark corners and beneath the chairs and spartan unused bed. The tablelamp burned fitfully, weak and tired. Even the fierce red eye of the coffeepot seemed diminished.

The admiral sighed, a pale, old sound, and stood up, stiffly, slowly, his arm cocked, the coffeecup in midair, only the cigarettesmoke moving in a languid curl. He was staring past the ensign out the terrace door.

The ensign stood too, surveying the room which was luxurious by hotel room standards yet was rendered anonymous and stark by the admiral's spare presence, the way he had of never seeming to live anyplace he happened to be but always someplace else. His homes, ten or fifteen over the past years of commissioned service, were that way too. He and his wife had completed entire tours in offbase housing without the neighbors ever knowing he lived there. He was neither secretive nor furtive, just tightly organized and regulation to the point of invisibility. The ensign could remember once many years ago overhearing his father say to his mother with unaccustomed petulance,

"What do you mean, have them over? They are *civilians*. What on earth would we talk about?" He was always at sea or at the office, living in a world within a world, as indelibly stamped physically and mentally now as if he were tattooed.

"So they are outcasts," the ensign said. "The officers. The crew."

"But, by God, they have a good time," the admiral said with surprising force.

"Wasn't it the Aztecs that used to do that? Take a few young people and give them the time of their lives for a while. Then sacrifice them?"

"What makes you say a thing like that? Sacrifice?"

"No, I mean, the young people didn't mind. They volunteered. They thought it was worth it, better than a long life with no fun, or something like that. Maybe I've still got the book, if you're interested, I'll—"

"Never mind. I don't wish to discuss the subject any more."

The ensign stared at the admiral. The way the morninglight hit him now he was a single shade of gray, flat, arid, and one-dimensional, unrelieved by angle or shadow: hair face beardstubble suit all stamped by the same cookie cutter out of pastrydough so thin and dry it would crack if moved.

So when finally the admiral moved the ensign was actually startled. But he only unplugged the coffeepot. The hot red eye winked out and the room was a single shade of gray dough, worn and thin. It smelled of stale cigarettesmoke and tasted of morningbreath.

"Wait—" the ensign said. "In *flagrante delicto*."

"What?"

"Jacqueline and Feldman. You said—found them in— that—'the report said.'"

"Oh. Yes."

"What report? Because you said he never turned them in."

The admiral was cleaning up. Fussily. The cups. The spoons. He spoke from the bathroom over watersplash and cupclink. "Not officially. No. But the word got out. Obviously."

"You mean one of the three—"

"Not necessarily." The admiral's voice was raised, distorted by the press and sound of an electric razor. "You know Bancroft Hall. It's not the most private—"

"My God. You don't mean—"

"The rest of the brigade."

"Why, my God!" the ensign cried, pacing now in something like shock. "An *exhibición!*"

"What?"

The ensign's voice climbed to a terrible and futile whine. "Like the houses here. I heard the sailors talking. They have whorehouses here—"

"*No!*"

"—where you can pay to see, to watch a man and a woman, no, not a woman, a—a whore. And a man. They—"

"Oh, I wouldn't go that far, Jimmie. They were all very young, and as innocent as you can be and still—"

The admiral reappeared, slapping his face vigorously, redolent of spicy aftershave, looking neat and fresh. He was putting on his jacket. He had probably changed his shirt. The ensign could never tell. All his shirts were identical white regulation and his soiled ones looked better than the ensign's fresh ones. He looked rested, fit, and ten years younger. He was carrying a small overnight bag.

"The report went to the superintendent of the Naval Academy. He wouldn't have minded pitching Murphy out. All he ever had going for him was good looks and a certain rough charm. He cheated a lot—"

"Sir! At the Naval Academy cheating is not tolerated."

"Getting caught at cheating is what is not tolerated. But if he kicked Murphy out he would have had to kick Orin Feldman out too and Feldman was one of the most brilliant midshipmen at the Academy. So he threw out the report instead."

"That's terrible. He ought to have been court-martialed. He ought to be found and court-martialed. He didn't do his duty."

"Not everybody does his duty always, Jimmie. Regardless of what we like to think. Well, it's certainly been good seeing you. Don't blame yourself for getting involved with the *Devilfish*. Everybody makes mistakes. Thing to do of course is straighten it out right away. You might as well fly back with me right now."

He had his hand on the ensign's shoulder, sweeping him along through the door. The ensign realized the admiral had checked out. All he had done in the room was shave, change his shirt, and have a cup of coffee. That was about all he had ever done in any civilian room he had ever occupied in his entire life. The room was immaculate, unused.

"I don't think I could do that, sir."

"Why not? I'll take care of everything, don't worry about a thing." He looked at his watch. "Plane is waiting. Car is right downstairs."

"I promised to take Mary Beth for—"

"Mary Beth will understand. She is a general's daughter. She understands duty."

"Duty means performing your assigned task even if you find it unpleasant."

"Come on. Don't worry. I'll take care of everything for you."

"That's just it. I don't want you to take care of everything. If you don't stop taking care of everything for me I'll just go on being Junior all my life."

"You stood one in your class, Jimmie. You did that all on your own."

"Book learning. There's more to the Navy than getting good grades. I'm going to stay aboard that submarine and prepare my report and buck it on up through Commodore Forbes."

"Forbes is the one who assigned you to the *Devilfish*, isn't he?"

"Yes, sir. He is the squadron commodore."

"Didn't it strike you as odd? The squadron commodore personally assigning an ensign to a submarine? Especially an ensign who'd never been to submarine school?"

"No, sir. I'm used to special treatment, being your son. Anyway, he said they needed me."

"Forbes has a devious mind."

"Are you trying to get me off that submarine because you're afraid if I follow in your footsteps I'll overshadow you? All your life you've sacrificed everything for your career and now you want to sacrifice me too—"

"Just shut up about sacrifice!"

"Dad—"

"*I want you off that submarine.*"

"Now, now, boys. Lower your voices. I could hear you clear down at my room."

"Well, Mary Beth," the admiral said. His cheeks were flushed. "You look fresh and rested. That's another new dress, isn't it?"

"This old thing? Just something I threw in my trunk at the last minute."

"Mary Beth brought a steamer trunk for the trip," the admiral said, looking at his watch. "Well, we better see about getting it loaded back on the plane. Jimmie isn't coming back with us."

"Then I'm not either, Admiral. My place is with the man I love." She put her arm through the ensign's.

"Very well, Mary Beth," the admiral said. "They don't make them that way any more, Jimmie. You're a lucky young man. Hope you appreciate it."

"Of *course* he does, Admiral."

"Show her the town. She's been reading up in all the guidebooks. You'll have a fine time. I envy you. Take her to the Tropicana tonight. Oh. Here's a little money. Till you, uh, get your wallet back."

"No, thank you, sir. I have to be back to the ship soon."

"I told you don't worry about that. I'll take care of—I spoke to your commanding officer. He tells me she definitely will not sail before tomorrow afternoon and that you are officially on liberty."

The admiral looked at Mary Beth, and something seemed to pass between them. Then the admiral was saying good-by and disappearing into the elevator holding his overnight bag.

"Let's go see the city," Mary Beth said.

"I'm awfully tired."

"Don't be selfish. I've never been to Havana before. Besides, I took a nap while you two were yakking away and I feel fine. Let's go." Mary Beth's father was a lieutenant general, and sometimes it was hard to tell who was which.

They engaged a taxi for the day and drove around Havana, looking at churches and parks and buildings of special architectural interest. Mary Beth had a guidebook open in her lap and gave a running description of the cultural offerings of the city.

"Jimmie, wake up. We're going to get out here. It's called Herman's, and the guidebook says they serve free frozen daiquiris while you shop for bargains in leather goods."

"I don't need any leather goods."

"Don't be selfish. I want to get a nice wallet to take back to Poppa. You ought to get him something too. Tighten your tie. Shouldn't you have worn your blouse? You look out of uniform."

"This is *Havana*, Mary Beth."

"Nonetheless it's a foreign port, and you should set an example for the natives."

Herman's was cool and inviting, and when the proprietor saw the ensign's uniform and Mary Beth's expensive Fifth Avenue frock he laid on the charm and the frozen daiquiris by the trayful.

"Well, we might as well take them. They're free. Take one, Jimmie."

"I'll have a Coke, thanks."

"They're simply delicious."

"Don't drink them too fast."

They had just bought their wallets when the peace of the establishment was rent by a gust of sailors sweeping in drunk and profane, grabbing the daiquiris from the tray, shouting at the proprietor, demanding to see things in the showcases.

"Did you see that, Jimmie? That sailor. He *stole* that watchband. He just put it in his pocket without paying. Call him over. Discipline him."

"Shhh. Let's go, Mary Beth."

"Don't shush me. Poppa says it's an officer's duty to—"

"Just don't attract their attention. Let's go."

"I got a dose," one of them said, drifting near to take more daiquiris from the new tray Herman set before them.

"You can't tell yet," his buddy said. "It takes a week."

"I could tell by the feel. She gimme a dose all right."

"Well, then you're lucky."

"*Lucky?* Listen, have you ever—"

"Sure. Now you can relax and enjoy yourself. You got nothing more to worry about."

"Young man," Mary Beth said. "Sailor. If you don't mind. Those are *our* daiquiris. They are for us, and furthermore—"

The sailor turned. "Lady, kiss my—hey! Looky here! It's Junior with some classy cunt! Hiya honey, any friend of Junior's is a friend of mine how about a little huh?"

They crowded around drunk holloweyed laughing shouting shoving shaking his hand heavily pawing her a little, though for them with a certain restraint.

"Like 'em flat-chested, huh, Junior? That's cause you're a *officer!*"

Then they were streaming out the door, waving, shouting, disappearing into the bright daylight outside.

"Well, I *never!*" Mary Beth said. She had another daiquiri, pale and trembling. "Mr. Herman please call the police at once. Jimmie, you should call the Shore Patrol. Did those creatures actually know you? Why didn't you do something? Did you *hear* that that thug calling you *Junior?* Why didn't you do something?"

"Like what?"

"Command them to be *civil*, show *respect.*"

"Oh boy. That would just have—"

"But you are an officer. They have to respect you."

"You have to earn that."

"No you do *not!* It is required by regulations. Poppa says so!"

"Better not drink any more of those things. It's hot and they're icy and they go to your head."

"Did you *recognize* any of them? Could you *identify* any of them?"

"Sure. They're all from my submarine."

"Are you *serious?* Your *shipmates?*"

"Mary Beth, I wouldn't joke about anything with you."

"One of them actually touched my breast. Could you identify him?"

"The one that said you were flat-chested?"

"Not that little idiot! The tall good-looking one, oh I think I'm going to cry . . ."

"Let's go, Mary Beth."

"We'll call your daddy. We'll call Poppa. They'll know what to do even if you don't."

8

In the cab she was sobbing so hard they missed several cultural landmarks. "Jimmie, I—they just ruined Havana for me. I don't want to sight see any more. I can't bear the thought that creatures like that are loose in the streets. Wearing the uniform of the United States Navy. Well, Poppa will hear about this, of that you can be sure. He's always said the Navy is very—*loose*."

"Of that I am sure."

"You better just take me back to the hotel now."

By the time he got her back up to her room she was disheveled, her hair coming loose, and she was having a little trouble walking.

"What did he mean a dose?" she said. "A dose of what?"

"Nothing. Never mind. Just lie down."

"You're not trying to take advantage of me, are you?"

"No."

"Just because I let you—you know. That once. Take my bra off?"

"You better take a little nap."

"You liked it, didn't you?"

"Yes. Very much."

"You know I'm not flat-chested."

"I'll give you a little neck rub."

"Mmmmm. That feels good. Oh, Jimmie, you'll make such a good husband."

"I'll just undo this, just a little. You'll be more comfortable."

"Make me comfortable, Jimmie. Those men were thoroughgoing vulgarians, weren't they? I can't bear the thought of you having to stay on the same ship with them. Especially that tall nice looking one who—I wouldn't trust him a minute. Do you know his name? Will you be able to ident—Jimm*ieeee*—what do you think you're doing?"

"Just hunch your shoulders forward a little, slip it off. You don't want to wrinkle it. Such a pretty dress."

She looked at him silently for quite a while, her face flushed. Then she got to her feet and undid her dress and let it fall to the floor. She stood then in an opaque full slip, staring at him with a funny look on her face.

"Shall I, Jimmie?"

"God, yes."

With a series of awkward nervous gestures she removed the slip and stepped toward him then remembered her new dress getting wrinkled on the floor. She stooped and picked it up and took it to the closet where she carefully hung it on a hanger along with her other clothes in their endless ranks and files.

She looked faintly pathetic, her prim walk unco-ordinated now and awkward, fumbling with the slip the dress the recalcitrant hangers. She was skinnier than he had realized or anyway allowed himself to notice, almost bottomless, her knees so knobby they nearly touched when she walked. They had little blue veins behind them. And the funny-looking little sailor had made a pretty accurate assessment.

"Darling," she said, "I guess you are sort of overwhelmed, but since we are going to be married in a few days anyway." She sat on his lap. "You need a bath. You smell funny."

"It's the submarine."

"I noticed it on those sailors, too, especially the one that—he had some kind of cologne on too. He thought it made him sexy, I suppose."

"You get used to it."

"He really thought he was sexy, didn't he? It's sickening. Those fellows. You know I actually feel sorry for them. You know what they dream about?"

"What?"

"Getting a girl like me in bed with them. You like that? Like me to do that?"

"Yes. *Yes.*"

"It's their fondest dream. Their lifetime's ambition. But of course they never realize it. Since time immemorial a lower-class male has considered an upper-class lady the absolute summit of his sexual ambition. That's why that big handsome idiot kept trying to feel my breasts. That isn't all he wanted to do to me either, you really like this?"

"Oh, honey."

"They're eating their hearts out right now wishing they were you. Do you appreciate me, Jimmie?"

"Sure. You know I do."

"Do I ever know you do—all those times in the car you tried to get me to put my hand there."

"Then how come you waited till now to put it there?"

"A man and wife can do things other people can't, I explained all that to you."

"We're not man and wife yet."

"We will be as soon as you finish nuclear-power school —ahh he really likes that, doesn't he? Ohhh, honey, he wants out shall I take him out, honey?"

"Ohhh, Mary Beth—I'm not sure I want to go to nuc—"

"There."

"*Honey.*"

"Isn't that better my *my*—now don't push, Jimmie, don't push me around."

"Thought you'd like to get comfortable."

"I am quite comfortable right here sitting just like this, thank you."

"But you—"

"*Don't*—we have to talk first."

"Talk?"

"You've simply got to go back home to nuclear-power school, Jimmie. Your daddy wants you to. My Poppa wants you to. And I want you to. Get off that horrid submarine. Those *creatures*—now don't push and maul me, Jimmie. You're just like them. It's coarsening, living among creatures like that. It's already had a bad influence on you. *Look* at me, look at *you*—this is awful. You ought to be ashamed of yourself."

"Well, don't stop what you started. At least do that for a change."

"I want your promise. It's bad for you. Associating with creatures like that. They aren't human."

"Mary Beth, those men were sailors in the United States Navy."

"Poppa says sailors are immoral, and obviously he's right. You don't have to deal with them. You shouldn't have anything to do with them."

"Somebody has to."

"Somebody else. Not you."

"Why not me?"

"Poppa has underlings deal with the enlisted men. He never has to talk to them."

"I don't have any underlings. I'm the underling."

"Oh, Jimmie, sometimes you make me sick. You can be so stubborn. You are meant for better things. High command."

"You mean you are. You're going to be a general some-day, Mary Beth."

"You've said that before and I know you think it's frightfully funny, but it's nothing to joke about. It's only natural that Poppa would expect me to marry someone with a brilliant future. I might as well tell you he'd much prefer me to be engaged to someone from the Point, but since you did stand one in your class and since you are going directly into the nuclear-power submarine program and since your daddy is an admiral, even if he is only a rear admiral—*isn't* that the funniest title in the whole wide world—*rear* ha ha admiral—"

"So he is going to give me a chance."

"Only if you go directly into the nuclear program. That's where the future admirals are going to come from. Everybody knows that."

"Even in the Army?"

"Jimmie, if he ever thought you were even considering throwing away your precious time in that lousy stinking diesel submarine with no future—oh dear. Look at that. He's gone away. My heavens what a change. He's awful *little*, Jimmie. Are you sure you're normal?"

"You know that sailor that put his hand on your tit?"

"Wha—that fellow in Herman's?"

"The tall, good-looking sailor?"

"What about him?"

"He's got one *this* big."

"*Honest?*"

"Famous throughout the fleet. Would you like to see it?"

She stared at him, eyes wide, mouth open. "How—*ohhhh*, Jimmie, you're *joking*. That's nothing to *joke* about hey wait, where do you think you're going?"

"I'm going back to that lousy stinking submarine with no future, Mary Beth."

"Wait *just* a *minute,* Jimmie Hillerby. You can't leave me like this—"

"Then get dressed."

"Stranded all by myself in a foreign seaport on a lousy stinking island with no way to get home."

She was standing, embracing herself, looking cold and awkward and mean in the sunny sensual hotel room.

He remembered abruptly the frustrating weekends at the Academy, the days of looking forward to a Saturday night date with Mary Beth, and the endless chain of endless scenes with the same sad ending. Now he noticed, amazed, that the immaculate impeccable scrupulous Mary Beth's impregnable panties were none too clean.

"James Hillerby! What are you laughing at? Oh you are the most infuriating—listen—don't you dare touch that door. You hear me? Poppa told me you weren't worth it! Ohhh God I should have listened to Poppa but when your poor father who is after all only a rear ha ha ha admiral pleaded with me to make this stupid trip to try to talk some sense into your stupid head I accommodated him because, well, after all my Poppa is a lieutenant general—"

"Lieutenant ha ha ha general."

"—and your daddy is after all only a rear admiral so I figured and Poppa concurred it was my *duty—*"

"*Noblesse oblige.*"

"All right, yes, if you want to put it that way. Now I can see you don't have any higher aspirations at all."

"You're probably right."

"All I want to do is get off this horrid island and away from the Navy scum that populates it and officers that allow them to run wild and insult ladies—"

"Go ahead. Nobody is stopping you."

He opened the door and just before he got it slammed behind him he heard her final shout:

"Poppa warned me about the Navy, you no good son of a bitch!—"

In the lobby he knew remorse. He went to the desk to explain that the lady was unexpectedly extending her stay another night. The clerk didn't even have to look up the room number, he knew the name.

"That is the general's daughter. She is reserved through tomorrow morning."

"She just call down?"

"No, sir. Say so when she move in."

"Well, anyway, she has a big steamer trunk and I better make arrangements to—"

"That's all taken care of too. Her father the general is sending a special plane down for her tomorrow morning." The clerk consulted a card. "You Ensign Hillerby? *Si.* I have ordered the car as well, as requested."

"By whom?"

"The admiral."

"For what?"

"Take the two of you to the airport tomorrow morning. Something wrong?"

"Everything's fine. But she'll be traveling alone."

The first person he saw on the submarine was the steward stretched out on a white Navy blanket on the after deck. He was wearing nothing but tan trunks which made him look naked. He was wearing huge sunglasses, reading a magazine, a bottle of rum beside him.

"Martinez."

"Sair?" Notmoving.

"Have you shined my shoes yet?"

"No sair," not even looking up.

"Why the hell not?"

"No time, sair. Too busy."

"Well, how about right now?"

"Oh no sair, not possible. Not feel well sair. Expose to terrible disease."

"Like what?"

"Syphilis, sair."

He looked up then and displayed for the ensign glistening white teeth and returned his attention to his magazine.

The ensign climbed down the forward torpedo room hatch. The door to the head was open and the captain was sitting there, his trousers around his ankles, a folded newspaper on his lap, smoking a slim cigar.

"Oh. Hullo there, Hillerby."

"Ensign Hillerby reporting for duty, sir." He snapped a regulation salute.

"Can you get back okay, kid?"

"Back, sir?"

"We are going to have to leave you here."

"Why?"

The captain shrugged, turning the paper over. "Admiral said you'd be leaving us. Sorry to see you go. You were going to be okay in time. Course, one thing we don't have much of these days is time."

The ensign protested in his voluble way, but the only answer he got to his reiterated *Why?* was a repeated *Ask your old man,* and finally, *Look, kid, I'm busy, okay?*

The ensign went into the forward battery and threw himself on his bunk in the six-man room. An immense fatigue overwhelmed him. He meant to get up, but he did not. He dreamed of Jacqueline so vividly he seemed to smell her perfume.

He was finally awakened by the distinctive motion of the submarine steaming surfaced in a long seaswell. He staggered out of the six-man room and into the wardroom across the passageway. The executive officer, smart and spruce in fresh starched khaki, was there. So was Jacqueline.

"Well, look who's here," the executive officer said. "I thought we put you ashore in Havana."

Beside the executive officer on the outboard transom seat Jacqueline drew her kimono closed and smiled tentatively. There was about the two of them an air at once domestic and serene. The wardroom was redolent of perfume, shaving lotion, freshbrewed coffee, frying bacon.

The ensign's mouth tasted like asbestos and he just stood there rubbing his chin. "I—I must have fallen asleep."

"You must be hungry," Jacqueline said. "Sit down."

"He's not even supposed to be here," the executive officer said.

"Well, neither am I. Get him some breakfast."

"Pantry! Ration of breakfast for the ensign."

Jazz music played softly over the intercom circuit. The submarine was moving with an eccentric corkscrewing motion, around, down, up and around again with unpredictable shimmers and lurches.

The ensign sat staring hard at the green baize tabletop. After a while a tan hand put a white cereal bowl filled with thick brownstuff before him.

"What's that?" the ensign said.

"Chili."

"Ohhh, he wanted some bacon and eggs, I'll bet," Jacqueline said.

"All out. Got no more."

The ensign breathed the leftover greasy chilismell and

the motion of the deck was translated to the pit of his stomach and then his throat.

"Why, you're turning green," Jacqueline said. "Maybe you better—"

"Scuse me!" the ensign said and he ran for the head, the executive officer's laughter ringing behind him.

They sat listening to his footsteps pound along the deck plates, heard him hit the loose plate by the coaming, heard his muffled cry as he bumped his head, heard the metal door to the head slam.

"He's cute," Jacqueline said. "He's so intense about everything."

"He's a pain in the ass."

The executive officer put two cigarettes in his mouth and looking into her eyes lighted them both and handed one to her. When he had first done that she had gone weak with adoration for his sophistication and charm. But she had been in high school then. Now he looked merely silly and she wished he wouldn't do it. It was embarrassing to take the cigarette looking deeply into his smoldering eyes, as if the transaction were somehow invested with unutterable significance. He took himself and everything he did very seriously. It was part of his charm. That and the foolhardy things he did which she understood now stemmed less from absolute bravery than from insufficient imagination to foresee the consequences.

"His old man is sure going to be sore when he finds out the kid is still aboard," the executive officer said. "He told Orin he wants him the hell off."

"Then why isn't he off?"

"Orin told him to get off. What more could he do?"

"You kidding? Plenty. If he really wanted him off."

The executive officer jetted smoke in a practiced heavy stream from his nostrils. Jacqueline had long thought that

one of the things that should appear in his Officers Qualification card was: SMOKES CIGARETTES SUPERBLY.

"We're lucky to scrape together enough people to take
this thing to sea every day. We need every hand we can
get. Orin says the kid is better than nothing. I don't agree,
but Orin's the skipper."

"Well then, the admiral will just have him transferred
off."

"No. Forbes says he stays. Orin called him. The commodore says unless the kid actually requests a transfer
officially, he stays. If the admiral wants him off he'll have
to do it through channels and Forbes knows the admiral
won't do that. He doesn't want any more attention paid to
this boat than he can help."

"Why?"

"He just doesn't. That's all."

"But why doesn't he? What does he care?"

"Special mission."

"Oh, for God's sake. You and Orin and your mysterious
special-mission talk. What kind of special mission would
anybody give this old tub?"

"You might just be surprised."

They had butted their cigarettes in the ash tray made
from a shell casing. Now he tapped his pack against the
heel of his hand in his practiced gesture that made two
cigarettes jump up just so and he put the two cigarettes in
his mouth, looking into her eyes, as with one hand he prepared the matchbook to light the match with his thumb
without even tearing the match out.

"Harold—*no*. Don't—"

"What?"

"Nothing. I—no thanks. I don't want one now. I just
put one out."

"What would you think of my career if I ended up with the Congressional Medal of Honor?"

She sat watching him smoke. He rarely joked about anything that big.

"The Medal of Honor?" she said carefully. "In peacetime? How—"

"War is where you find it."

"What is that supposed to mean?"

"It could lead to flag rank. A Medal of Honor. Couldn't it?"

"I suppose it could, yes."

"You bet your lovely ass it could," he said, jetting smoke. "But you got to be aggressive to get your medal, your command, your flag . . ."

Command. Flag rank. She thought he had gotten all that out of his mind long ago, but lately somewhere somehow somebody had been dangling things before him he was not really equipped to handle, and now it had all come back worse than before, all the business they had fed him at the Academy and he had swallowed hook line and sinker: that his chances were as good as anyone else's to make admiral. She had liked him best, felt most comfortable with him, when he had seemed to accept the inevitable, that with luck he would retire as a captain, but most probably as a commander—and possibly not even quite that. He had always been dangerous when filled with too much ambition.

"I suppose this has something to do with your big secret mission," she said. "Where does Orin figure in it?"

"Oh, he is the CO, of course, but like I said, they don't pass the big ones out like popcorn. Orin isn't quite aggressive enough. He thinks too much. He'll probably get a Navy Cross or something like that."

He thought a minute, examining his cigarette, letting

smoke out his mouth and inhaling it through his nostrils. He had spent an entire evening once teaching her to do that. She had been dizzy and impressed, but even then she had thought, *There must be something else he is good at.*

"I'll tell you this, Jackie. With no war on, it's our only chance."

She patted his hand where it lay on the green baize table cover. "How about a game of acey-deucy?"

"Great!"

"And you can tell me about the new car you're going to get."

"Ohhhh, some sweet deal," he said, exhaling smoke. "Is that ever some sweet deal. Listen, I'll start at the front bumper and describe every chrome-plated nut and bolt in that machine, that is some sweet chariot . . ."

"You do that," she said, listening for the ensign's footsteps, following with her ears the dejected tread as he approached, watching him look mournfully in, then slink on across the way to his bunk.

9

When they returned to Key West the ensign devoted himself to the submarine with the singular concentration that had made him number one in his class at the Academy. The study of the submarine was the kind of problem he was very good at: mechanical, finite, contained. You did this, and that happened. If it didn't, you used the back-up system. He was not really amazed yet that people could not be handled this way, just puzzled: he had not yet fully discovered they could not. He still thought he must be just pushing the wrong buttons.

He traced out the submarine's muscles and sinews with the dedication of a surgeon. He diagramed the main hydraulic system, the electrical systems, the ventilation system, the refrigeration and air-conditioning systems, the trim and drain system, the blow and vent system.

The crew stumbled over him at odd hours, flashlight in one hand, a volume of the ship's plans in the other, poking and probing making notes and sketches. He would be crawling around the forward torpedo tubes one day, the after tubes the next.

"You're liable to find him anywhere," Sprague said. "You got to watch out you don't step on him."

"You know what gets me?" the mustang said. "The look of ecstasy on his face."

"Of what?"

"Ecstasy. You know, like the boat was a woman and he's about to come."

Sprague rubbed his scalp with his thick fingers. "You're sick, you know that Foster, don't ya? Sick."

"Me? Why me? It's him. He's gone ape over—" He said the name but it was lost in Sprague's heavy hawking. Sprague spat on the deck right in the middle of the passageway, right in the middle of officers' country, right at the mustang's feet.

"Clean that up! I'm a officer and that's an order!"

Sprague only glared at him. "Balls. You're just a warmed-over engineman." He stepped over the yellow-green glob and went on.

"Martinez!" the mustang said. "Come here on the double and clean up this mess!"

Martinez's voice, sleepy and mean, came from the tiny serving pantry next to the wardroom where he perched on an upended bucket, a magazine open on his knees. "Clean it up yourself. Your fault anyway."

The mustang went to the pantry door and stood glaring in. Martinez held up a butcher knife, grinning with his teeth though not with his eyes. The mustang went away.

The *Devilfish* went to sea daily and daily returned through the tortuous doglegged channel, though the ensign no longer stood on the bridge shouting out his memorized courses. He was at various stations through the submarine working on his Qualification notebook. If the *Devilfish* was waiting for something, was on short-notice standby alert, it did not affect the ensign. He had only to find the day's assigned op area on the chart then ask Sprague to lay off the track to it. Sprague would always have done this before he was asked, unless he had been cruising the Duval Street bars the night before, in which case the ensign did it himself. He still thought he was going to submarine school any day. It was a pleasant enough life.

The *Devilfish* drew daily the close-in operating areas, the ones that lay just off the channel entrance, thus were reached with relative ease and speed. Assignment to these areas was coveted by married skippers whose wives and families were in Key West. Out to the near op areas each morning and back to the pier each afternoon with time in the long southern evenings for golf or gardening gave the naval profession the comforts of a nine-to-five civilian job with credit for sea duty into the bargain.

It could grow on you, it was something like yachting, seductive and soft, leaving for war maneuvers already thinking of cocktailtime and dinnerguests or games with the kiddies. More than one career had been hurt by the tropical life that Key West and the near op areas could provide.

So once you got the lush duty you had to fight it, beware of succumbing, the way the British colonials carefully dressed for dinner and had all manner of ceremony in their little jungle outposts to keep from going native. Commanding officers like Spunky Waters did this, and you could see the crews lined up on the forecastle each day, going out and coming in, in clean whites, hats squared and (the *Devilfish* crew reported in awe: it was common gossip) *shoes shined!* The other submarines held emergency drills too.

"That's what we should do," the ensign said, wiping grease from his nose with his sleeve, his other arm straight out lost in the maze of piping aft of number four engine, one foot cocked over the other, peculiarly (for him anyway) at ease.

"What is?" Sprague said. "We ought to do what?"

"Hold emergency drills."

"Why?"

Sprague had been passing by. Now he stood poised as if in midstep, immobile but tense, springlike, thickbodied but neat, quartermasterly with his clean dungarees and T shirt, braided white lanyard around his sunburned neck, stopwatch pendant on his barrelchest. There was the air of the bridge and conning tower about him, brisk, clean, and quiet. Except for the round white hat clamped on the back of his head, he might have been a high school football coach on his way to practice. He seemed out of place down here in the belly of the submarine in the roaring heat and greasy ambiance of the engine room. The ensign in his soiled torn khaki, the greasy rag drooping from a back pocket, looked more at home than Sprague did. The ensign shrugged.

"Because we are a man of war—"

"We're a submarine!"

"—and our purpose is to make war! So we're—"

"That's where you're wrong! If you think—"

They had to shout at the top of their voices against the sound of the engines.

Braaaoooooooga! Braaaaoooooga! The diving klaxon sounded and the mustang's voice electronically boosted to sound even more like Donald Duck cried *Dive! Dive!* over the 1 m.c.

Instantly the ensign's hand shot up to a lever which he yanked, bending, putting his body into it performing an interlocking series of quick precise movements which produced a great sighing *whooosh,* and the engine stopped. A sailor performed a similar dance on the neighboring engine, and then the ensign and the sailor moved in concert back and forth between the great silent engines and the ensign nodded and the sailor jerked a telephone from its cradle and said,

"After engine room engines secured," just as the deck pitched sharply forward and a jolt of air hit their eardrums like giant fingers squeezing sharply.

The sudden silence was eerie. "It spooks me to be back here when we dive!" Sprague said, still shouting. "You can't see anything and it's so damn noisy."

"Not now," the ensign said. "Very peaceful and quiet."

"That's worse. After the noise. You sure you guys didn't forget anything?"

"Everything's fine," the ensign said.

"Well, I got to get back to the bridge. Just came down to take a leak."

"The head is forward."

"Yeah. Well, it was full. I had to use the one aft."

"Sprague, you don't have to apologize to me for walking through the boat. You don't have to explain."

"I ain't apologizing to nobody for Godsakes what's the matter with you. What's to explain?"

"You want to take a leak, take a leak. That's your business. Of course now if you were spying on me, trying to follow me around, why, that would be different."

"Who'd want to follow you around? Why'd anybody want to do that for?"

"I've been wondering the same thing. Because every time I turn around you're about two feet away."

With the engines shut down, the engine room watch had little to do but wait around to start them again. The sailors twisted into positions of ease among the machinery, arms and hands jutting at strange angles, holding paperbackbooks, magazines with pictures of athletes or naked women, cigarettes, cigars, candybars. The abrupt and total cessation of engineroar made the ears throb and seem to sting. The silence was absolute, eerie; men who had had to hold their mouths to each other's ear and shout to be understood now heard easily the striking of a match, the conversation of sailors at the far end of the compartment.

The deck slanted down and they were conscious of the rustle of dark water all around them. An invisible force assaulted the air and Sprague grabbed his ears. "What the devil is that?"

"Negative venting inboard, that's all."

"Oh."

"Happens every dive. I should have thought by now you'd—"

"I know I told you I *know*. It's just that I'm never back here where you can't see or hear nothin' don't know what's going on. It's spooky. You sure everything's buttoned up good and tight down here?"

"Back here. We're not any deeper in the water than the control room is. In fact with this down angle we're shallower than the conning tower."

"I know. Feels like it though."

Sprague had gathered himself tensely and seemed to be trying to extend himself in all directions look everywhichway at once as if the very fact of vigilance might somehow keep out the water.

Why, he is scared, the ensign thought, remembering that he had heard about people like that: flyers whose knees trembled on the way to the airplane, surgeons to whom blood was nauseating, deep-sea divers who paled and swooned as the helmet was lowered, sea captains who grew seasick at the sound of the engines starting. To these people apparently the feat itself was attractive, differing in dimension but not in kind from the attraction more normal citizens find in roller coasters, parachute jumps, and driving too fast for conditions.

He is probably always a little scared in the conning

tower too, the ensign thought, *but he has learned to handle it there because everything is familiar and all the apparatus for control is there and the periscope to see outside with and the captain or executive officer nearby* (*it's okay, Daddy is here, he won't let anything go wrong and he'll fix it if it does*), *but back here he is in a more foreign land than even I am,* the ensign thought, *because so far this is all I know.*

"Ignorance is kind of a help sometimes," the ensign said.

"Huh? What'd ya mean by a crack like that?"

"It was the fish, wasn't it?"

"What fish?"

The ensign looked at Sprague who had not moved and stood in complete and awesome immobility listening to the thick silence. They were moving more deeply into the belly of the sea but the light stayed the same.

"You know very well what I'm talking about. We are engaged in practice maneuvers daily but we aren't carrying practice fish. We have warheads in tubes one and two. *Why?*"

Something sprang loose in Sprague, and he turned, looking from the ensign to the heavy watertight doors at either end of the compartment. "Leave it alone, will you! Just quit poking around. You're getting on everybody's nerves! Everybody's got enough to worry about without worrying about you too. Anyhow, you ain't the inspector general, you know. Who the hell do you think you are! I don't care who your daddy is—"

They were leveling off now. The motion of the deck seemed to reassure him. His voice dropped off in mid-shout, though the other sailors in the compartment continued to watch him closely. There was in their attitude the lynxlike air of jungle predators, and the compartment of cold efficient light, all gray and white with red handles or gauge wheels here and there (beware: hands off), took on an ominous, haunted air.

"It was all there like one big sweet dream," Sprague said. He hadn't moved. He seemed to have been transformed into a terrible and profound immobility. "What in the hell happened? I was going to be a chief. Could have been, too. Could of made it easy. But always some piece of cunt comes along or maybe a couple a drinks too many here and there but it always come back to the fuckin women and what do I have to show for it? Half a dozen doses and things they don't even know I got because nobody ever had 'em before. Souvenirs of foreign travel, ya might say. You don't get no ribbons for that. Promotions neither. Ruined by a hard on, is what. Attacked by my own prick. That's what they ought to give me. A cocksman's badge. A great big cock on a ribbon to wear instead of a chief's hat. No. It'd look like a prick in a bandage and I already got that. What they ought to gimme is a navy issue solid gold cunt guaranteed sanitary, a GI cunt which—who the hell's got the dive?"

Because now the deck lurched abruptly up. There was no depth gauge there, but the enginemen could estimate the depth accurately enough by reading the water pressure gauge for the main engine salt water intake.

"Going up in a hell of a hurry," a sailor said. "Maybe they spotted it."

"Not here," another said. "No chance."

"Spotted what?" the ensign cried. "You—"

"Who's got the dive?" Sprague said. "Must be the lousy mustang."

A sailor snatched a phone from its bracket on the bulkhead and called and asked control and slammed it back in the bracket and said, "Right, Sprague. It's him. You recognized his touch."

"It figures," Sprague said. "He drives it like a wild horse." Now they lurched down again and conversation started but the downangle held too long and conversation stopped and they froze just staring at each other and the ensign wondered what he as the senior and only officer present should do. What do you do in the after engine room to keep the ship from sinking? Then they felt the air hit outside. High-pressure air struck the mass of solid water in the after ballast tanks as indubitably it was striking simultaneously the water in the forward tanks.

"He blew safety too!" a sailor said, replacing the phone.

"Who did?" Sprague called. "Not the mustang. He wouldn't have the sense."

"Capm did."

"Yeah."

The submarine shuddered and strained as the air slammed against the water packed in the ballast tanks hard as cement at this depth. Then it gave, and the deck started up beneath their feet, canted in a peculiarly cattywhompus fashion as the submarine lifted corklike and uncontrolled toward the surface. They felt quite clearly the instant of broaching, the change in the quality of motion as the submarine broke the surface and entered the world of air and gravity.

The low-pressure blowers started. Only then did the surfacing alarm sound, anticlimactic and somehow forlorn as the enginemen and the ensign scrambled around to obey the 1 m.c. command in the captain's tin voice to stand by to answer bells on two main engines. They stood transfixed, looking at each other. The ensign saw that Sprague's T shirt was now sweatsplotched. His own was too, and his shorts were suspiciously damp.

So I am not used to it yet, he thought. *Maybe you never get used to it.*

They could tell when the conning tower hatch was cracked all through the submarine. The inside air pressure dropped abruptly. As soon as it did and they felt the submarine safely cradled in the surface wave troughs, Sprague sprinted forward.

Something in the rigid celerity with which he ran arrested the ensign's attention and he fumbled in his attempt to get the engine started with the smooth swinging grace of the resident engineman.

"Wait for Chrissakes!" the sailor said. "He only said stand by—"

But the ensign was gone too, running after Sprague.

The distant wheeze of the low-pressure blowers increased to a blurred roar as he made his way forward through the forward engine room, the after battery with its closely ranked tiers of bunks in dimness, the illuminated tables of the crew's messroom, and finally the Times Square and Grand Central Station of the submarine, the control room.

The control room was all tense efficiency submerged, but now, on the surface, the huge green divingplane wheels abandoned, the blow and vent manifold secured except for the vent on safety tank, which was still flooding, the large central room its bulkheads encrusted with thick junglegrowths of pipes wires gauges handles valvewheels dials and warnings engraved in brass seemed chaotic and disorganized with sailors moving this way and that yelling at one another and from above the distinctive smell of fresh sea air and the unmistakable aura of sunshine.

He made his way up the conning tower ladder bump-

ing his head against the bottom of a sailor already mid-
way down.

"Junior, for God's sake, why don't you watch—"

"What's going on?"

"We surfaced."

"No, I mean, why?"

"Scuse me would you please sir if you don't have no
fuckin objection I been on watch and it's time for chow,"
muscling on down and by, backing the ensign off the
ladder, riding his head down with his rear end.

Holding the rail as if to keep his place impatiently the
ensign waited a break in the downstream of sailors then
made his way up the ladder and into the conning tower.
The search radar was manned and the periscopes, normally housed upon surfacing, were both up and manned,
searching in different directions. At the big sonar console
by the ladder to the upper conning tower hatch an old
chief in a dress blue uniform wearing huge foam-rubber
earphones that made him look like Mickey Mouse
hunched over the gear, eyes squinted in concentration,
only the very tips of his great thick fingers moving as he
nursed the small training wheel through its practiced arcs.

The cramped conning tower was now like an attic with
a skylight, the great upper hatch lid cocked open by its
giant spring and held secure by its latch, vertical, serene,
with the same air of tensely coiled immobility the sonarman had.

The engines still had not been started. The submarine
lay dead in the water wallowing now in the long gentle
swells, imparting to the supine and powerless hull almost
no pitch but a profound and stomachchurning roll, very
deep and remoseless, from this side to that, the sound of
falling pots and pans and breaking crockery filtering up

from the crew's dinette aft and the officers' pantry forward.

"Permission to come up on the bridge, sir!" the ensign bawled, head back, hand to mouth, already starting up the ladder when the shout came back, "Not now! Stay below!"

The ensign went on up anyway, tensed for a foot on his head or shoulder, but nobody even noticed him. They were all standing against the bridge cowl, glasses to their faces, staring out over the starboard bow. The executive officer was pointing.

"That's where the son of a bitch went down. See there?"

"Nawww," the captain said. "You can't be sure."

"We don't have time to be sure," the executive officer said.

"We don't have time for anything else," the captain said. Still neither lowered his glasses.

It was the ensign himself staring in the other direction who shouted, "Periscope! Periscope!" and then he said, "Is that what you're looking for?"

They swung around, focusing their glasses on the periscope feather. Sprague was up on the turtleback with two lookouts, all with binoculars, and they were all shouting excitedly now too.

"Quiet on the bridge," the captain shouted.

The executive officer leaned over and pushed the button on the 7 m.c. "Stand by to answer bells on the battery. Secure the engines. Stand by to dive."

"No, wait," the captain said, very stiff and tense. "We have to be more sure."

"Well, my God—"

"Why all the excitement about a periscope?" the ensign said. "We see them all the time out here."

For the first time the captain lowered his binoculars

and looked around at the ensign. His eyes were hollow and forlorn, very deep and dead with purple smudges beneath them. "Not this one, we don't," he said. And then he said, "If it's the one we think it is."

"Of course it is," the executive officer said. He shouted down the hatch, "On the TDC! Here's the setup—"

"No, no," the captain said.

"I'm just setting up. We've got to be ready."

The captain didn't say any more and the executive officer went ahead with the setup, calling down the estimated course and speed of the periscope. "Angle on the bow port forty. Estimated range one oh double oh."

"Sonar contact!" a voice with the timbre of rusted iron bawled up the hatch. The captain whirled at once to kneel over the hatch facing down. "Shift to—" he said and then shouted louder to penetrate the Mickey Mouse earphones of foam rubber. "Shift to the speaker!" The old chief incongruously natty in his dress blues reached up and flicked the switch. The steady beat of the submarine screws announced itself whirling in ambient watersound.

Everyone strained to listen, staring down the hatch as if they would somehow be able to see the submarine's sonar signature. Sprague had his stop watch going, tapping it with his forefinger in rhythm with the sonar beat.

"That's it!" he announced.

"You sure?" the captain said.

"Of course he's sure," the executive officer said.

"Pretty sure," Sprague said. "I mean, it certainly could be."

"You guys are like one big itchy trigger finger," the captain said.

"Jesus, Orin," the executive officer said. "It's got to be him. Who else could it be? There is nobody assigned to that area. Let's shoot him and get it over with."

"Like one big itchy something or other," Sprague said. "Not trigger finger exactly."

"Before he shoots us," the executive officer said. Which had some effect on the lookouts, young sailors, one with a bad left eye all squinty (*A lookout!* the ensign cried to himself: *a lookout with one bad eye*), the other with scars crisscrossing his cheek and throat.

"Yeah for God's sake let's sink the commie prick and get outta here!" one shouted.

"Shut up," Sprague said.

"It's my ass too, ya know," the sailor said.

"It's your ass anyway if the captain sends ya back where you come from," Sprague said, not even shouting now, just exasperated, as if the conversation were an old and familiar one. The sailor said no more but glared with his one good eye through his binoculars at the periscope feather.

"Generating!" came up the hatch from the TDC.

"Come on," the executive officer said. "We'll have a solution in a minute. This may be our only chance. Let's get the goddam job done."

"You sure nobody is in that area?"

"Absolutely. We checked it. And the nearest boundary is two miles the other way. Anybody in there has got to be after us."

"Then why doesn't he dive? Go deep?"

"Because he's doing what we're doing. Getting a solution."

The captain stood immobile, his glasses hanging against his barrelchest, staring at the surface of the sea and its invisible secrets. Then he leaned to the 7 m.c. and pushed the button.

"Stand by tubes forward," he said.

They rode on in tense silence, the water rushing at the

hull, the tank tops, waves echoing hollowly against the air-filled ballast tanks. Only then did the ensign realize they were running on the battery, had swung around and were heading for the periscope.

"It will be a nice shot," Sprague said. "Right up his ass."

"Must be something wrong, he can't shoot," the scarface lookout said. His voice shook, and when Sprague looked up at him, the lookout said, "Well, dammit, I'm looking right at his eyeball."

The periscope had turned, was looking directly at them, an opaque and baleful eye on a metal stalk thrust up from the deep, trailing a feather of spume. Each man on the bridge was free to examine his own soul and wonder what the brain behind the eye beneath the magnifying mirrors of the periscope was even now deciding. Or had already decided.

"Orin," the executive officer said. "You better open the tube doors. He's closing us!"

"Open the outer doors!" the captain said.

"Open the outer doors forward!" Sprague shouted down the hatch.

"Open the outer doors forward aye!" came back at once. And then very quickly, "Outer doors ford are open!"

"Stand by one," the captain said. "Final bearing and shoot. Set depth forty, speed high. Take the bearing from the number two scope. Radar, can you get a final range on his scope?"

"Eight hunnert yards!"

"Ready—"

"Check fire! Check fire!" It was the ensign.

They were all so intent on the firing solution or just staring transfixed at the periscope through their glasses the ensign was the only one to notice at first.

"What the hell?" the captain said.

"He's broaching!" the ensign cried, pointing. "Lookie!"

"So what?" the executive officer said. "Maybe he's surfacing to shoot. All the more reason to—"

"Wait a minute," the captain said. "He is coming up all right. Check fire down there; wait."

"God damn it," the executive officer said. "Shoot him now. Don't wait till he's got positive buoyancy. We've got to—"

"Wait."

Transfixed, in eerie silence they glided through the translucent water, closing the range. The gurgle of high-pressure air bubbling from beneath the tank floods was clearly audible now.

"He sure came up in a hurry," the executive officer said. "Coming right this way." He spoke to deathly silence. He slapped his pockets, which sounded very loud, and found a cigarette. He hunched his shoulders over the wind whipped flame of his windproof Zippo, pulling the smoke in deeply with a grimace. He jetted smoke from his nostrils looking at his wristwatch. Then he saw the ensign staring at him.

"Well?" he said. "What's on your mind, Junior?"

Because everyone else was still staring at the wet gray conning tower across the wedge of water, staring at the large white numbers on the sail.

"Who is it?" an old man's voice said, and the ensign had to look to see that it was the captain speaking.

"That is Captain Waters' boat, sir," a subordinately respectful and chastened voice said, and the ensign looked over and saw that it was Sprague.

"Whaduhyaknow," the captain said. "Spunky Waters."

They all stood watching. An air of endless and desperate waiting settled heavily upon them.

"All stop," the ensign said down the hatch, not his voice, his father's voice, full of brisk command. Nobody said anything. Bells jangled below.

"Answers all stop, sir."

"Very well." There had never been any engine noise. Now the quiet forwardthrust ceased.

"Losing steerageway, sir."

"Very well."

There was a metallic bang, very loud across the narrowed band of water, as the upper conning tower hatch flew open and locked. They wallowed in the water, watching.

"There he is," somebody said.

"There's Spunky," the captain said.

"That is the commanding officer himself, sir," Sprague said.

Both *Devilfish* periscopes were trained on him. Three, four, half a dozen sailors had drifted up through the lower hatch without asking permission and now stood goggle-eyed, staring across at the other submarine. From Spunky Waters' point of view it must have looked like a cartoon with more heads than the tiny bridge could accommodate, all staring silently over at him.

"Well . . ." the captain said under his breath, the single word very old and tired. "That does it. That's it."

"Leave it to me," the executive officer said.

"Leave what to you? You awready—"

"*Shhh.* See what he has to say."

The *Devilfish* fell again into the long troughs, rolling heavily as the other submarine drew abreast. They could hear the whine of low-pressure blowers.

"He's got his glasses on us," Sprague reported though they could all plainly see him. "And here comes his quartermaster up with the book."

"He isn't looking it up," the executive officer said. "He knows our number by heart. He is only verifying it."

Spunky Waters shouted across the water then: "Feldman? Murphy? What the hell are you crazy bastards doing anyway? You opened your outer doors, didn't you? Is that what we heard? You're mixed up, aren't you?"

The captain only stared wide-eyed and forlorn.

"About what?" the executive officer shouted. "Maybe you are!"

The distance between the submarines had closed until it was hardly twenty or thirty yards. They occupied neighboring troughs, rolling now toward each other now away. The heads on the opposite bridge seemed to sink and emerge from the shimmering crests.

"Oh no. I got the op plan right here . . . *I'm* supposed to make the approach on *you* . . . I had a perfect solution generating and then sonar reported you were opening your outer doors. So I came up. Hell. If we both shoot it's —well, there's no such exercise, for one thing."

The captain found his voice and said, "Spunk—" but the executive officer was angrily shouting.

"Gawd damn it, Spunky, you are out of position again!"

"What?"

"You are in the wrong area!" He was shaking a piece of paper Sprague had just handed him. "You are assigned to area—" He told him the number. "That's two miles *that* way!" waving and pointing angrily like a farmer on a country road arguing with an ignorant tourist as Spunky Waters and his gathering contingent of officers sank beneath the wave tops and reappeared and sank again and bobbed back up. They were consulting books and papers and charts over there. Spunky Waters' voice could be heard shouting at his own crew. Then he was up on the turtleback holding on with one hand, a loudhailer in the other. He didn't need it. It blasted their ears.

"Sorry guys! We ran out of our area submerged. We're supposed to be working with . . . another boat . . . disciplinary action here . . . can be sure." He waved. Only Sprague waved back.

Smoothly the submarines drew apart and took divergent courses. The captain stayed in his cabin with the curtain drawn, while the executive officer played acey-deucy with the mustang all the way in. The ensign could hear their shouts of laughter as he perched on a stack of BuSanda manuals and, using his bunk for a table, began to enter the endless stream of corrections on the navigational charts.

10

It was the middle of the day. They came in anyway, docking so early there were no line handlers. The captain stayed below and told the executive officer to make the landing. There was no problem getting a berthing spot along the normally crowded waterfront. Most of the submarines were still at sea. The executive officer didn't even radio ahead. He just went up for the landing, picked the empty pier nearest his car, drove her in until the sailors could leap over with the lines, tied up, and declared liberty.

"Base Radio is raising hell," Sprague said. "They say we are in somebody else's space. They say we have to—"

"Tell Base Radio to go screw—" the executive officer said, and walked over the brow, hands in his pockets, cigarette in his mouth, not even saluting the quarterdeck. He got in his convertible and drove off.

The ensign stationed himself at the brow as O.O.D., since no one else did. To give the offgoing sailors somebody neat and military to salute. Few saluted either him or the national ensign aft, and when finally he looked it wasn't even up. He just walked off the submarine then.

So now I'm doing it too, he thought. *Well, it's what everybody else does. Just walk away.*

He walked as the executive officer had, his hands in his pockets, hat low over his eyes, not saluting.

On dry land he walked rapidly, but he had nowhere to go and abruptly he missed the submarine. He felt like a small boy playing truant and pushed on for approximately the same reasons a small boy would. There was a peculiar holiday air about being off the submarine, ambling about in the middle of a working day.

The submarine was where he went to school now and he was playing hooky. He had never done that before. A slow-moving car honked and honked again and he waved his fist without looking up, cursing, and ambled on. There was something going on inside him, but he could not get it to focus.

T shirts. He needed T shirts. He ambled over toward small stores. It gave him something to do. The familiar sign seemed a personal affront:

CLOSED FOR INVENTORY.

Why are those always hand-lettered signs? he thought. *They ought to paint that on the door when they built the building, then nail it shut. How come they were always taking inventory when they were never open long enough to sell anything?*

He thought to go to the Navy Exchange (*For what?* he thought *for what?*) or the gedunk stand or, no—the B.O.Q. was in the other direction. He maintained a room there, his nominal home, his because he had the key and kept a shaving kit and change of clothes there and parked his car there.

He would take a drive. And as soon as the thought surfaced he had a goal: Arlington, Virginia, to see Mary Beth. And as soon as he thought of that, the maelstrom inside him had its focus. He knew then what was bothering him, making him a little woozy in the tropical heat, making the clammy feel of his sweaty clothing and the slick dampness of the sweatband in his officer's hat an offense against his flesh.

He walked on and the walking itself, the pull and tug of his damp shirt and trousers, was an embarrassment, an announcement of his loneliness. He thought of the girl in Havana. A passing sailor saluted, and the ensign, usually the most punctilious of salute returners, the very personification of absolute military courtesy, removed his hand from his pocket long enough to wave, nod, and mumble "Hi."

There were two B.O.Q. buildings: the one which housed the ensign's shaving kit, and the one across the street. The one across the street had flag quarters, senior officer quarters and a small officers' club, which is to say a bar.

The bar was called the Echoasis and the ensign had been in it once or twice for a beer. Parked in front of the Echoasis was a yellow Jaguar. The ensign noticed it because it was so cavalierly parked in the middle of the curb space marked NO PARKING ANY TIME. He thought the club might be closed until early evening when most of the submarines would be in, but an officer staggered out blinking and shading his eyes and disappeared into the shimmering heat, so he went on in.

It was a small, rectangular room with chairs and tables, the angularity relieved by a bar with four or five barstools at the far end. The ensign knew this but could not see it. The club was merely pleasantly dim, but after the blaze of sun on the white streets outside it was black as night and the ensign stood blinded. The room was airconditioned heavily, so dry and icy crisp it took his breath away.

He knew where the bar was and stumbled toward it. Then he saw her, seated on a high stool, her elbows on the bar before her one forearm straight up the hand straight up the two fingers holding the cigarette straight up the cigarette a slash of white against the ambient dark.

She took shape in her sheer white blouse like the magical effect in the movie fantasy where the body materializes out of thin air against a background sketchy and dim. He even heard the offscreen romantic music but soon realized it was a radio in some anonymous B.O.Q. room somewhere beyond the thin wall behind the bar. What lonely bachelor lay there in his stifling room listening to the radio? What were his thoughts?

"Sit down," she said in a voice cool, dry, and dark as the air.

"What? Oh. No. I. I have to be going—"

"I almost ran over you, you know. I honked and wanted to give you a lift but you wouldn't even look up. I figured you were going to meet your girl somewhere. What's her name?"

"I don't have a girl."

"Mary something? She was in the plane with us going over to Havana. Your dad said you're going to get married."

"What in the world would you two talk about?"

"Oh, can she talk? She stuck her nose in a book and didn't say a word all the way across. After she told us her father was a general."

"That's Mary Beth."

"You live here?"

"Across the street."

"I thought you were heading here so I came right here, but I was about to give up."

He could see her better now. Not the face the actual features yet the thin white blouse had a life of its own it was sleeveless the smoothwhite arms tapered just so the long white fingers toyed pinktipped with her glass her cigarette he thought he could see through her blouse.

"Give what up?" he said.

"Well, where the hell have you been?"

"Look, Mrs. Feldman—"

"I told you to call me Jacqueline. I told you that that night you came by to pay your duty call on your new commanding officer and he wasn't even there."

"No. Well—" the ensign shrugged. He felt solitary and chill, a statue, thicktongued, tremblefingered.

"So all you found was what you thought was his wife entertaining a—a what would you call him?"

"Friend."

"A friend. And you never told."

"Maybe."

"I would have known in ten minutes if you'd ever told. Told anybody in the Navy anyway. Morals are funny, you know. Those who most vigorously oppose our—what would you call it?"

"Relationship."

"Relationship would be the first to make the most of even the tiniest violation of it."

"How? Make the most of it how?"

"By telling Orin or Murph of course. Or the squadron commodore. Oh, I can read your expression. I know what you're thinking. But it isn't true. They are quite jealous of anybody else."

"But the commodore—"

"He hates the very idea but he hates the idea of any violation of it even more. I guess you might say he has swallowed all he can swallow and one tiny bit more and he will strangle on his own rage, so, no you didn't tell anybody and I like that. Discreet. That's how you can tell a gentleman."

He could see her face now, very pale and fine, soft-glowing. *She certainly manages to stay out of the sun,* he thought. He heard her voice accompanied by machinery-noise and blowerwhoosh saying, *I'm air-conditioned* and saw her going up the ladder disappearing head bosom hips legs into blinding sunlight.

"To reappear here," he said.

"Discretion is—what?"

"You disappeared into sunlight, so naturally now you reappear from the afternoon sun."

"You stood first in your class. That's really something. I didn't mean to kid you about it."

The bartender was an off-duty sailor in a red aloha shirt, the blue tattoos on his forearms strangely lumines-cent in the dim light. He appeared and placed before the ensign a tall, icy replica of her drink which she, not he, had ordered with a single motion of a single finger and a slight inclination of her head, and retreated to his chair at one of the tables where he hunched over a maga-zine without nearly enough light moving his lips slowly.

"What's this?" he said.

"Singapore sling."

"What?"

"Crazy, but they taste good. You'll like it. Go a*head.*"

"I am kind of thirsty. All that walking. Gosh. Must be over a hundred out there."

"Better than beer and not so fattening. Well. So tell me. Quit beating around the bush. What the hell hap-pened out there? I've been to the boat. Murph wasn't aboard and Orin wouldn't talk to me."

"Well, you could always try Sprague."

"Oh, so you've heard about that too." She looked at

him with that hot, bright regard. He waited, strangely uncurious, unbreathing, remote. Who after all was she to him and why should he care at all about her tangled past? Except that it wasn't even past, it was present, and in just talking to her he was part of it. He quenched his thirst at the icy liquid, anonymous and uplifting. He propped his arms against the bar.

"None of my business," he said.

"Sprague was—you know Sprague. Big puppydog. He's just a friend now." She studied him as if to see whether he believed this or whether he cared, he could not tell which.

"Yes," he said. "Well . . ."

"He wouldn't talk to me either. Just wouldn't talk about it. There's a limit to how long I'll chase men through that submarine. I've got my pride too. But I want to know what happened. They have a fight or something? They've been coming close to it lately."

He took a long pull at his drink, not looking at her, aware of her glance at his cheek. He looked beyond her to where the bartender sat some distance away at his table, immersed in his magazine, reading silently word by word.

"They—we almost sank a submarine."

"*What?*"

"It was Captain Waters' submarine, they—they were about to fire when he surfaced. He'd heard our outer doors open, I guess, and he got suspicious. Or scared."

"Spunky? You almost sank Spunky? Are you sure?"

"Sure I'm sure. I was working around the forward torpedo tubes and just by chance I discovered tubes one and two are loaded with warshots. You understand what I'm saying? Warheads. So of course if we'd hit him, he—"

"No, no, I mean you're sure it was Spunky?"

"Sure. Why? What difference does that make?" And now it was his turn for outrage. His voice rose. "It was a submarine. That's all. If we are going to go around playing real war we can't shoot at anyone we don't mean to sink. Can we?"

"Oh, you poor honey. No wonder everybody was so upset. And you're sure it was Spunky? Yes. I can tell. You're sure. Well. That explains it. Mac. *Mac!* Bring us another round here."

"Why would we carry warshots?"

"You wouldn't. I'm sure you're mistaken about that."

He didn't say anything.

After a while she said, "Did Orin and Murphy—did they have an argument over this? Words?"

"How should I know?"

"I thought you were there."

"The captain went to his cabin and didn't come out and Mr.—"

"And Murph laughed and joked and was pretty loud and boisterous all the way in."

"How'd you know that?"

"It's his style. He's always that way when he fumbles. Every time he makes a mistake he gets that way. Only of course there is no way of knowing whether he figures the mistake was in almost sinking Spunky's boat or in not getting the trigger pulled before he surfaced. He really hates Spunky."

"If that's a joke it isn't very funny."

"No. I guess not. I'm sorry." She stared hard at her drink, touching a fingertip in and out of it. "When do you go to sea again?"

"I don't know. You never know. Nobody ever seems to say anything. They just—see, what I want to do is hold regular quarters every morning, muster, make announcements to the—"

"Day after tamorra."

"What?" Jacqueline said. "What was that?"

Solitary and squat, stolid in the icy air the bartender jerked a thumb toward the ensign. "His boat. It sails day after tamorra. One of the crew was in just before ya come in. Said the Old Man wants that word put out."

The ensign sat staring with that air of terrific amazement. "So that's how they communicate. They just get it out of the air like a flock of birds. They don't even—"

"Why?" she said. "Why are they in port tomorrow, Mac?"

"Engine trouble."

"What?" the ensign cried. "What? We didn't have any engine trouble!"

"Engine trouble, sonny," the bartender said. "Don't fight it." He returned to his table and his magazine.

"Never mind," she said. "Don't take it so hard. He shouldn't have talked to you like that."

"It's all right. They all do it."

"No, it's not all right. You mustn't let them. You call him right over and—"

"It isn't him that matters. It's them. I've got to be going."

"Where you going?"

"I've got things to do. I only came in to cool off."

"Oh. I thought maybe you saw my car."

"It's so darn hot out. I'm not used to the weather yet."

"Me neither. I just avoid it."

"Oh, that's right. You're air-conditioned."

"Why don't you have one for the road?"

"How many of those have you had?"

"No, really, I just sat down when you got here."

"They kind of hit you in this heat."

"Not in here."

They had one for the road.

He helped her off the barstool and they were both a little unsteady. The bartender waved away the ensign's fivedollarbill. "On the house for Jacqueline, sonny, and any friend of hers. Not that that would cover the check anyway." He watched them disappear through the door.

The heat was bad. After the chill dimness of the bar the sunstruck day was a physical assault. They stood blinded, unable to think. She had neither hat nor sunglasses.

"My car," she said. "It was right there. It's those marines. They've towed it away again. Isn't that awful? I was hardly in there a minute. Wait till Orin hears about this."

The heat grasped the ensign, choking him, hitting him hard at the temples, everything a white blaze. He shielded his eyes, looking at her. She had not moved. She seemed strangely defenseless devoid of glasses, parasol, car. He fancied he could see her beginning to burn.

Gravely he handed her his hat and gravely she accepted it. Still they didn't move.

"My car is in the parking lot over there," he said. "I can't even see it, I can't see across the street, but I know it's there. I'll be glad to take you wherever you want to go." He felt a rush of giddiness and the prospect of walking across the street seemed suddenly the culmination of a lifetime's ambition. He might manage that but nothing more.

"Look," he said, "if you don't want to walk I'll be glad to go get the car and pick you up."

"Don't leave me here, for God's sake. I'll turn into a piece of mahogany. I'll look like a Conch."

He realized they were in the middle of the street making their way across as carefully (looking thisway looking thatway) as if there were heavy and dangerous traffic though the hot white street had the air of a stretch of desert, nothing moving anywhere. They gained the sidewalk and then were before the big white building. He didn't realize they were holding hands until he tried to let go.

"Look, the car's another hundred yards. Why don't you go on in the lobby and sit down."

"God it's hot. It makes you dizzy. How many of those things did we have?"

"Too many. You go sit down. I'll go get—"

"Okay. And turn on the air conditioning."

"Turn on—my car isn't air-conditioned."

"It isn't? My God. It'll be worse inside than out."

She, they, did not stop their slow forward motion. There was at least the suspicion that if they did they would never move again.

"Only for a while. I'll open the windows—"

"Never. I'd rather die. In fact, if I don't sit down soon, I will."

They were in the lobby. A steward's mate glanced sleepily over, went back to his paperwork. A lieutenant with a great shock of red hair sprawled obscenely in a wicker chair, sleeping noisily. An ancient gent in civilian clothes, a camera around his neck, sat writing endless postcards, a reserve officer on two weeks' training duty. Other than that there was only the empty lobby, the collection of rickety nondescript old furniture and the stifling heat. Overhead one of those old ceiling fans that look like the propeller from some airplane that has crashed straight down through the roof languidly revolved packing more tightly the thick, oppressive air.

"I really feel faint."

"Sit down."

"If I stay in here one more minute I—if there was just one decent fan you could stand in front of—"

"I've got two fans in my room."

"Real genuine electric fans?"

"Sure. Bought 'em myself at the Navy Exchange."

They were already moving a little faster, they each staggered a little, they bumped in the hallway and he put his arm around her to steady her or himself he was not sure.

It was a small room with an upper and lower bunk, a chest of drawers, a washbasin, a small desk and a single chair.

"I've got to use the head," she said. "Excuse me."

"There isn't any."

"Don't be ridiculous."

"No. Honest. It's down the hall."

"I know that. I saw the sign. Right back."

"You can't do that—"

"You want me to use your basin?"

She was wearing white linen slacks. She put her hands to the zipper at the side and he felt everything leap and pound within him.

"I'll go check," he said.

"There's nobody around."

"Never can tell."

He led the way, entered, and had only opened the door to check the first stall when she entered the second. He saw her feet, saw the slacks gather around her ankles as she dropped them enough for her purpose. He retreated to stand guard at the door, hearing clearly the domestic and intimate tinkling sound.

"Wait! You can't go in there!"

"Why the hell not?" It was the lieutenant from the

lobby, tall, redheaded, and sleepy, already unzipping. He shoved past the ensign and settled himself at the urinal, feet spread, elbows out, head down.

He was just finishing up, fannyback, arm moving, when Jacqueline appeared behind him. "Give it a shake for me, honey," she said, and joined the ensign fastwalking down the hall.

Inside the room they stood awkwardly. There were no drapes and the room was absolutely bare except for the mirror over the basin and a single picture torn from a cheap magazine and Scotch-taped to the wall.

"Who's she?"

"Who—oh, *that*—" He leaped up and tore it down, crumpling it, kneading it fiercely into a hard little ball. "I —that must have been here when I moved in. I guess I never noticed it."

"I guess you never did all right. You can see it from the bed can't you? What are you going to do now that it's gone? You'll have to find somebody real."

"Oh, I've got a girl. Lots of girls."

"Yeah, well if they're all like Mary What'shername you're better off with pictures. Which is your bunk? This one here? Who sleeps up there?"

"Nobody. I don't have a roommate."

"So neat. So nicely made up."

"The stewards do that."

"Mind if I sit on it? I won't muss it or anything."

She sat on the lower bunk. He perched on the edge of the only chair.

"It's not so bad in here with the shades drawn and those fans going," she said.

"At night it's not so bad."

"What do you call that? That the fan does."

"The fan does? What? Go around?"

"Vibrate?" She moved her finger in a circle.

"Oscillate."

"Oscillate. Can you fix it so it doesn't oscillate but just blows straight on me?"

He got up and went to the fan and found the little knurled knob and turned it and aimed the fan right at her. She sat basking kittenlike in the breeze, moving slightly this way and that. She reached with both hands behind her head and pulled her hair up and rubbed the back of her neck.

"That's where you really get hot," she said.

She let her head hang way forward between her knees and tried to get the effect of the fan on the nape of her neck. It was very white and soft, an intimate glimpse of naked womanflesh and the ensign found its casual presentation in the close shadowy room terribly disturbing and connected somehow with the implied soft outcurve of her flanks where she sat on his bunk and the way her breasts were defined when she tossed her head up and smoothed back her loose strawcolored hair with her hands just sitting there like that a while looking at him immobile and somehow frightening so that again he dropped his glance and studied his feet and then hers.

Her feet were bare in high-heeled sandals, the only part of her even lightly suntanned, the toenails painted soft-pink like her fingernails, a fragile golden chain around her ankle. He was studying the anklet when it disappeared the slacks crumpling down around it obscuring the shoes too and part of the floor.

She worked calmly, rationing her movements, not looking at him. She removed the white linen slacks without standing, seated on the bunk in the current of warm air the fan provided, mottled softly by striations of light and dark from the venetian blinds rolling slightly from one side to the other moving them down and finally off experiencing some difficulty with the shoes which she did not remove.

"You want to do this or shall I?" she said, indicating the buttons on her blouse.

He sat crouched forward on the chair animallike all feet and hands, unable to move. He did not trust his hands or the strain of movement. He said something, tried to speak, but his tongue was thick, dry, actually trembling.

"Iiiiahhhee—"

She looked at him. "Well?"

Again he made the same sound. She smiled and kept looking at him and his eyes felt locked in hers. He tried to look away but he could not as smiling looking at him she worked calmly directly down her front then rounded her shoulders and behind her too and straightened so that just beneath his line of vision peripheral soft and light-mottled her breasts appeared nipples punctuating a gathering force immobile and profound.

They moved. His vision seemed as if it might break if he looked where he wanted to. He stared straight ahead. Her breasts appeared directly in his gaze then passed rising as she stood.

Her panties were white, he could see that, because now he was looking everywhere, punctuated with surprising darkness just there so that he thought with wild irrelevance *so the sun that tanned her feet has lightened her hair too*. His glance, stare, was frantic now, pressurized by the focusing of his need. There was within him the pressure of a time bomb ticking, a vicious cycle of tightening constricting spiral, the pressure itself adding pressure until he was frantic his very frantic terror the final unbearable—no.

Her leg was. The inner part of it. The way so casually
she presented it as she (her thumb hooked in them) began casually to work them down. He was transmogrified,
became in the instant the silky nylon wisp gathering beneath her thumbs, fingers, moving down, caressing the
sulky flesh as she wiggled slightly in accommodation, the
very casual subtleness of the movements unbearable, and
something else: their history: the inescapable realization
of all the times she had removed them thus before he even
knew she existed, and after he had met her too indubitably
and when? and where? and for whom? and of all the times
too she would do so in the future without his being there
or even knowing about it, which, the not knowing, would
be even worse. So in the instant of standing and reaching
he understood for the first time truly the incredible sym-
biotic bond of Murphy and Feldman.

Stand and reach was all he did. All he did that she
could see. The rest only he knew in the instant of straining
shudder, the ecstatic ooze the more explosive because
despised, unsought. So that once its unmistakable tension was announced his every muscle ligament sinew and
brain cell clamped down hard against it exacerbating the
very reaction he tried so desperately to deny.

"What's the matter?" she said. "You all right? You look
sick." She did not sit but remained standing, stepping out
with one foot, raising the other foot to remove the garment
with her hand. She did not cross the foot to the knee but
did it the other way, simply raised the knee angling it
out as she reached toward the shoe where they dangled,
a revelation so casually explicit his final defense crum-
bled and he gave himself up to himself moaning.

"What?"

"Nothing." He made an unintelligible sound, his body
frozen in mortification.

"Well?"

She had not moved, her immobility terrible and calculated. Then she started toward him, an incredible sight, the apotheosis of his every youngman's dream. She took the three or four steps, everything subtly moving, wearing only the high-heeled sandals. He thought his heart would break: everything he had ever wanted within his grasp but denied him, short-circuited by an erratic connection between imagination and reality.

He would remember those few steps even after future events redressed the outrage: never again would a woman be that desirable that close that unobtainable.

She embraced him and he would forever recall that too: transformed again becoming now her flesh and feeling in a strange reversal the course texture of his khaki shirt and trousers against her warm bare flesh. Then she touched him.

"*Honey,*" she said. "You *didn't.*"

He stood speechless, impuissant, loathsome to his own thought, his hands to his face.

"I'm sorry."

"*Sorry.* He's *sorry!* Well if this isn't the *damnedest* the *God-*damnedest—"

She was in furious motion, this way and that, everything moving, trembling. He realized for the first time she was wearing little gold earrings that shimmered. And the damned high-heeled open-toe sandals. She was more erotic than ever now in her anger, a caged beastie wild with frustration.

"I'm sorry, Jackie."

"You said that."

"What can I do?"

"Do? You did. Have fun? Enjoy yourself? Of all the damned—"

She grabbed her clothes at random, righting, rejecting, flinging down, expressing her fury. She didn't even put her bra on, just her white blouse, then stood arranging her hair before the mirror over the basin, arms elevated pulling at her hair, breasts shadowy beneath the sheer white blouse, naked beneath that down to the high-heeled sandals which, the heel of one, caught in the white panties as, standing on one foot, hopping angrily, she tried to get them on, ripped them, gave up, cursing, and tossed them at the wastebasket where they draped over the edge.

"Well?" she said. "Well goddam it don't just stand there gawking. Give me a cigarette. Call the marines and get my car back."

"I—I don't smoke."

She was pulling her hair back hard, her hands up and behind her doing something to her hair. She stopped what she was doing, staring at him as if he had just entered the room.

"Get out."

"But I—"

"You're embarrassing me."

"No, I—"

"Then I will." She marched to the door just as she was and swung it open.

"All right," he said. "I'm going."

He walked on through, brushing by her, trying to collect himself. The big redheaded lieutenant was just outside in the passageway in an attitude of patient and expectant waiting. His eyes widened. His mouth opened.

"I'll get some cigarettes," the ensign called. "Close the door."

"Cigarettes?" the lieutenant said. "You want a cigarette?"

"Never mind," the ensign said.

"I'm talking to the lady."

"Thanks," the ensign heard and saw the lieutenant's arm outstretched, and hers.

"Light?" the lieutenant said.

"Mmmhmm. Thanks. Go 'way now." The door slammed.

In the far corner of the lobby was a telephone booth and into this the ensign plunged clashing the accordion-door behind him as the little domelight came on to burn peevish and pointless overhead. A tattered green base directory hung from a string. Fumbling, the ensign found the motor pool number, dialed, the plastic instrument sweatslippery in his hand, listened to the rhythmic bleat of the busy signal, hung up, and furiously dialed again (thinking: *Some sailor talking to his girl friend you'd think they'd have something better to do tend to business my God do you suppose he actually saw her there standing like—how could he not?*).

"Hullo?" he bawled. "Lissen whatsabigidea talking all morning listen I want to—want to—listen you got to bring her car back—what? What's the what?"

He did not know the license number or base tag number or if it even had a base tag and he could no longer even remember what it looked like. He thought of simply describing Jacqueline nude to the insolent sailor on the grounds that most of the men in the world must have seen her that way at one time or another, why not him? But he didn't say anything, just jammed the perfidious instrument back on the hook.

Because through the little window in the stifling booth he saw Jacqueline sweeping across the lobby, bouncing in her sheer white blouse, the white linen slacks obscene to the experienced and knowledgeable eye, the redheaded lieutenant striding beside her (looking goggle-eyed at her up and down) now moving swiftly ahead of her actually running out into the parking lot, the sweat springing in great dark patches at his back as if he were wounded and bleeding.

He is, the ensign thought. *But he doesn't even know it yet.*

He calculated with his eye the possibility of catching up to her, trying to imagine what on earth he would do or say. Standing, an intimate feeling of glue and starch immobilized him; in the instant of pause he lived the entire episode over, trying to make it come out differently.

Once he got moving it was not so bad, bearable, the physical part anyway. But by then she was stepping into the car, a large, long Buick with greentinted windows and an air-conditioned look, the redhaired lieutenant smugly at the wheel leaning across to open the door. Then they were pulling off, the ensign in the doorway of the B.O.Q. looking after them.

"Goldbricking s.o.b.!" shaking his fist. "Why isn't he at sea or in his office *doing* something instead of just hanging around—ought to be protective legislation. I got to take a shower."

But he returned to the telephone booth (it smelled, strangely, of her) and assaulted furiously the dial already shouting as the operator came on the line.

"—get to the bottom of all this, stop all this! They can't —he can't—"

"—umber are you calling sir?"

"Pentagon. Washington, D.C. Wanna speak—"

"—ust a moment, sir. The charge will—"

"Charge?" the ensign shrieked. "Not me. *He'll* pay!"

An hour later he left for Washington, D.C.

11

"So you see, Jimmie, we have to sink that submarine."

"But that would mean war."

"Not if we do it right."

The admiral stood poised in lightglow, heavy with gold braid and decorations. The downfunneled light cast his eyes in shadow: his eyes seemed to be missing, as if the admiral were staring out at him through macabre holes, stygian, proud, and uncaring.

"*Right?*" the ensign cried. "*Right?* My God, a foreign man o' war with a full crew and you are trying to tell me there is a right—"

"In our waters, Jimmie. Don't forget that. He is not supposed to be there. No right. No right to—"

"International waters. He is in international waters. We don't own the Caribbean—"

"This is no time for legal technicalities. They are in our waters, as far as I am concerned, any time they are cruising the Caribbean on the surface let alone submerged. We tolerate it on the surface because it is out in the open. You let a man carry a shotgun down the street. You don't like it but you let him because you can watch him. Cruising the Caribbean submerged is like going around with a concealed weapon. You can't do that. You don't do that. Everybody knows that. Sooner or later they will sink one of our—"

"No! That's impossible. That would mean war. They know that as well as we do."

"Is that what you want, war?"

"Well, if they sunk one of our ships certainly—"

"Even if there were a better way?"

The admiral stood surrounded by the panoply of his rank, the great desk, the huge globe with its miniature mountains and valleys and endless seas, the flags, the photographs and paintings of ships and seascapes and naval heroes, and everywhere the plaques, the testimonies, the ornate mahoganymounted insignia of the units, the ships the divisions the squadrons and fleets and finally the staffs he had commanded. He was a large man, but very neat and tidy. Busy. He had just left a meeting and was on his way to another. His heavy cap with its encrustation of golden rank lay on top of his slim leather briefcase on a special little table by the door. Large paintings of sea scenes were tastefully framed.

Yet the office had a bleak and impersonal look, cold and unlived in, like a well-maintained and authentically detailed museum room. It was unrelieved by even the coffee maker. He didn't need that here. He had installed outside in the outer office a coffee facility so comprehensive a casual visitor might have thought the main business of naval officers was the production of coffee rather than its consumption.

"But this is all conjecture," the ensign said. "You can't read their minds, no matter how ominous it looks. So they have a submarine operating in the Caribbean. Okay, even buying your argument that it is there illegally, you still don't really know they will use it to sink any of our ships. If they did that we would go right to war with them. They know that. That's what it's all about, the guided missiles,

the Strategic Air Command perpetually airborne, everything—our bases abroad. You can't just—"

"Jimmie—"

The ensign paused, turning, waiting for the rest. The
admiral had aged years since Havana. His voice was old
and tired, so soft suddenly he had to say it twice before
the ensign heard it or anyway understood it.

"They already have, Jimmie."

"Have what?"

"Sunk not one of our ships but two. Two new nukes.
Waited for them and got them submerged . . . bang!"
The admiral held up his hand and aimed his forefinger at
the wall, cocking his thumb down over it. "Just like that.
Fish in a rain barrel. Nobody the wiser."

The ensign sprang to his feet, shouting not so much at
the admiral now as at the huge chart of the Caribbean
which covered an entire wall.

"Wait! They couldn't get away with that! If they did
something like that the whole world would know."

"The whole world does know, Jimmie. They just don't
know how it happened. Who did it."

"You don't mean—you aren't saying—"

"That's right. Those are the boats."

"But they collapsed. They collapsed when they ex-
ceeded test depth. That's what the papers said. That's
what the *Navy* said."

"It's accurate enough, as far as it goes. The question
is: why did they exceed test depth? What made them
sink?"

"Well, the papers said . . . the papers said—"

"Yes, all right. What did the papers say?"

Infinite fragments of headline paragraph column brilliant indepthanalysis sepulchral televisiontone surfaced
at once in the ensign's mind, moiling. He realized he had

been thinking of that for some time now not in any certain way just vaguely the way you suck and pull at the idea of your own death without ever getting it up to the surface of your own mind where you can really see it.

"Nothing," the ensign said. "It was in all the papers and on the television but there wasn't any real answer. Just a lot of speculation and double-talk. Navy is investigating, they said. Possibility of crew failure, they said, structural failure, they—"

"Yes. They got that from the stories of air crashes. Sounds astute. And it's always a possibility of course."

"But in this instance it wasn't?"

"Unless you want to say it was crew failure because they failed to protect themselves from enemy attack in the Caribbean submerged. Which is what some of our military and congressional leaders are willing to say. After all, they say, what good is a nuclear submarine if she can't protect herself from attack. They've been saying that about our aircraft carriers for years too. You know the line. Why bother to build them if somebody might sink them."

"But my God—that means—that means she can just pick off our entire submarine fleet one by one."

The admiral shrugged and lighted a cigarette at the end of his ivory holder, snapping shut his engraved Zippo with an expansive gesture. "She might. She could, I suppose, though by then even Congress might get suspicious, take action. No, I think they don't want war. This way is better. She will just cripple our nuclear submarine fleet. Just quietly and economically decimate it. Just sink a boat every once in a while, one here, one there, a couple at a time now and then. Then Congress will say, what the hell, why bother to let you guys keep building those things if all they are going to do is go to sea and sink. Better give the money to the air force."

"But how are you going to find her?"

"We have pretty good intelligence on her. We have tracked her. We know she was in the vicinity when those two nuke boats went down. We know her habits now. It's like watching a shark. She hangs around the entrance to Gitmo a lot. Then she prowls our nuke transit lanes in the Caribbean. Lately she's been nosing around off Key West. Very deep water there. She's looking for victims again, Jimmie. Somebody has to stop her. And that somebody has to be the *Devilfish*."

"Impossible."

"Difficult."

"Not the *Devilfish*. They'll never do it, for God's sake. Not that bunch. Not them in that ancient rust bucket. It's a suicide mission."

"Jimmie, I am not asking you to get off because I think you are scared."

"I know that. I appreciate that. And I'm not. I'm not scared of taking a reasonable chance. But what's the point in going out with those bums in that stinking submersible sewer pipe to get sunk without a trace and for what? Just nothing at all. Somebody else will still have to go out and get the job done."

"No. There won't be any second chance. You have no idea what I've had to do just to get the *Devilfish* on this, just to get two warheads out of the ordnance system without the whole Navy knowing where they were going and what they were for, just to keep that submarine free of routine commitments that couldn't be overridden without explanation up and down the chain of command, just to collect a crew that's—"

"Expendable."

"All right. Yes. It's the waste. I don't want to waste you. There are other jobs for you to do. Later. Grand career ahead of you. This mission is for people who have already had their chance—people we, well—people we can afford to lose. Can you understand that?"

"Listen, nobody wants to see a ship lost. But if we have to lose one, that is the one to lose."

"You will get off then?"

"As soon as I get back."

"Don't even go back aboard. Go right to Commodore Forbes and tell him you have decided to request a transfer off, because you are going to nuclear-power school. He can't stop you, but he might delay you. And if he does I want you on the beach, not on the boat. This commie submarine is sniffing around in the Gulf somewhere and as soon as we can get a decent fix on her we are going to send the *Devilfish* out after her fast."

"You've had false alarms before, I think. That's what that Havana trip was all about, wasn't it?"

"That's why I flew the captain down. I thought he would get a crack at her off Gitmo, but she disappeared again. We won't lose her next time. Good-by, Jimmie. I have a meeting—"

"Soon as I get back, sir. And thanks."

12

When he returned to Key West he went directly to the B.O.Q. and checked out. Lugging his suitcase, he headed for the squadron commodore's office, walking along the waterfront.

There the *Devilfish* lay, mostly submerged, low and grim in the water, moored alone at a pier while the other submarines were in cozy nests. She looked forlorn and abandoned, ignored by her more respectable sisters as if somehow they sensed her impending doom and abhorred her very presence. He felt a sudden and surprising rush of affection for her. At least he could say a quiet good-by.

He struggled his suitcase over the brow and stood on the deck breathing in the familiar submarine smell (stench, Mary Beth would have said) of diesel oil and batterygas and cooking chili coming out of the main induction. He knew where the main induction valve was, and how it operated and where everything else was and how it all operated and he was struck with an idiotic sense of affection for the intricate doomed and obsolete hulk which he knew now like the back of his hand.

It was very hot in the sun. His uniform was already sweatstained from the walk from the B.O.Q. carrying his bag. He knew inside it would be cool. He was struck as he opened the forward torpedo room hatch by the abrupt and incongruous sensation of luxury and ease below as the heavy air conditioning reached up for him.

He left his bag on the deck, he would only be a minute, and worked his way down into the upper escape trunk and closed the hatch over his head, turning the dogging wheel the careful half turn sufficient to hold the hatch on the latch but leave it easy to open for the next person. The submarine routine was an interlocking complex of such small courtesies, the observance of some a matter of life and death, and he was touched and impressed by this more today than he ever had been before.

He dropped through the escape trunk lower hatch and down the ladder to the padded green deck of the forward torpedo room. A sailor was working on the number four torpedo tube and the great bronze door stood open, a yawning cavity in the nose of the submarine. The doors to tubes one and two were firmly shut and locked: behind them live torpedoes waiting to be delivered futilely against an impregnable target by an expendable crew.

The sailor whistled softly as he worked with rag, oilcan, and wrench, nodding absently at the ensign in the shared camaraderie of the deep. He didn't even know the sailor's name, but there was something between them that existed between few other men because together they went to sea in submarines.

The ensign moved aft through the cool compartment in its eternal even light, a scene of bunks and torpedoes and intricate order he had come to know so well. Still he had the sensation of rushing downhill, events out of control now proceeding of their own momentum, and he knew he would not be able to halt them until he had left the submarine and transferred to nuclear school, never to see the rusty old diesel boats again except from a distance, as curiosities, manned by their archaic crews.

He stopped to use the head, not because he had to but
because he enjoyed the small neat engineering problem
of valvewheels flapperhandles and gauges required to
perform even the simplest act inside a submarine even on
the surface, thinking (as he operated the flapper and
opened the sea valve, closed the sea valve, closed the
inboard stop, and closed the flapper, checking carefully
the pressure gauge for number one sanitary) that of course
only a small part of the submarine ever surfaced anyway:
the very deck on which he walked so securely and com-
fortably was under water now and had been since the
ship was commissioned and would be until she was
scrapped.

The submarine was an intricate arrangement of inter-
dependent parts all carefully balanced in a perpetual
state of internal tension with a certain fierce beauty like
an expensive watch in a case of steel, everything dependent on everything else. When everything worked well it
was an engineer's dream; when even the smallest thing
went wrong, a nightmare. With a rush of pride he realized
that he was now one of those who knew how to make
things work right.

He moved on aft through the heavy watertight door
and into the forward battery and stepped into the officers'
pantry just to prolong the moment of leaving. All he could
find in the little refrigerator was a container of ice cream,
mostly empty, and some bottles of beer.

He went into the wardroom and poured himself a cup
of coffee and sat down in the captain's place at the head
of the empty table in the empty wardroom and found himself just across the narrow passageway from Jacqueline.
She was sitting at the small pulldown desk in the captain's
stateroom, looking over at him.

"So there you are," she said. "I've been looking all over

for you. I was just writing you a note. I've been worried
sick about you."

"A lot you care."

"That business in the B.O.Q.—I'm sorry. I was—I don't
know. Can you ever forgive me?"

"I—I don't know."

"Really? You don't know? Well, you better make up
your mind and you better make it up right now. I acted
like a bitch because that's what I am. A bitch. I may be
tired of all that now and want to change, leave it all behind me, but I don't apologize for it and you might as
well know what you are getting. A bitch." She was crying,
luminous eyes in her pale drawn face.

He stepped across the narrow passageway and entered
the little stateroom and drew the curtain and immediately
they were isolated, contained in their own private capsule
within the larger enclosed capsule that was the submarine's pressure hull, encysted, protected from the rest of
the world by thick hatches, watertight doors and twenty-
oneinch torpedo tubes fore and aft. Softly the blowers
forced air around. Her hair was soft to his touch.

"I know," he said. "I know all about you."

"No. Not all. But some. And do you like it?"

"No. No, I don't like all of it."

She patted his hand. "Good. You're honest. So that's
something we have in common. I don't like a lot of it
either. But I'm not ashamed, I'm not apologizing, I—"

"I know. You said that. You don't have to apologize
because you don't have anything to apologize for."

He was standing beside her chair and in the little stateroom there was scarcely room to lean over. She put both
her arms around his hips hugging him, her face against
his khaki stomach. "Well, anyway, nobody can ever blackmail me. I certainly don't have any secrets."

She wore a wraparound dress of some sort, not yellow for a change, a kind of dark purple. It gave a little with the curve of her shoulders and he could see the white swell of her breasts.

"There's one I'd like to know about," he said.

She looked up at him, littlegirlish and guileless. "All right. We can have my big confession now if you like. I'm willing to do that. I want to, for you. I really meant that about the blackmail; I don't want some idiot to surprise you someday all unawares by—"

"I don't care about any of that. I just want to know about that redheaded lieutenant yesterday."

"Well, I'm afraid you picked a dull one for openers. He was taking me to the motor compound to pick up my car. I figured that's where they'd hauled it, they always do. But we didn't even get that far. The marines picked him up right away. He'd had some trouble with them and they were laying for him. He wasn't supposed to leave the B.O.Q."

"I'm glad to know that. You get your car back?"

"Yes. I knew one of the marines . . ."

He leaned to kiss her hair but there was not even room to bend over that much very easily. He stood holding her, smelling her, feeling her face against his stomach, looking from her golden hair to the green curtain that separated them from the world outside.

"Now. Where do you want me to start?"

"I don't. You just finished."

He raised her then easily and with one hand folded up the desk and gently and almost automatically she stood and embraced him not merely suffering the vigor of his embrace against her softness but augmenting it with thrust and tension of her own. He sat on the bunk and she sat beside him, very close, sometimes her head on his shoulder sometimes kissing his cheek his ear or being kissed.

The wraparound dress of dark purple turned black as he snapped off the light and for a long while stood holding her head her shoulders smelling her feeling her face her cheek against him, listening to the *whoosh* of air from the blowers the casual footsteps moving by in the passageway the timbre of sailorvoices talking in the tiny ship's office just aft over the desultory tap tap tap taptap of the typewriter (not the yeoman's practiced touch: some sailor writing to his girl or—strangely enough a lot of them did, often asking the ensign how to spell certain words—his mother).

He moved her back and down then, easily and gently, naturally, simply lifting and guiding with his hands as she responded neither eager nor reticent just agreeable, almost automatically it came so naturally. There was a comfortable domestic air about it, at least at first, as if after years of marriage they had come down to the submarine to rediscover their passion.

The compartment was at first very dark though gradually relieved by the sliver of light from the passageway over and beneath the curtain. When finally he undid the single tie and opened the dress, black now in the dark, she lay all white luminescent skin framed by the dress, like drapery it became, on this side and that, against which the light from the passageway illuminated gently the throat the breasts the round soft belly the quietly waiting thighs their dark punctuation revealed as two hands his and hers worked at the tiny nylon pants, black this time, not white.

She moved easily, domestically, unwantonly, accommodating more than enticing, wifely and serene, competent more than passionate, helpful and friendly, accepting.

Undemanding unchallenging undemonstrative she accepted first with fingertips then with dark punctuation then with slight lift and gentle thrust the fine confident column, enveloping it within her, secret and hidden, his, hers, invisible from all the world their shared and silent secret protected by the armor and might of the U. S. Navy. A sailor went by keys and tools jinglejangling footsteps growing and diminishing aft. Something was dropped against a metal deck plate forward and a sailor swore. A small yard vessel of some sort came close aboard and veered off, the sound of its propeller surprisingly clear through the hull.

"What's that?" she said. "That throbbing noise?"

"Nothing. A tug. Going away now."

"Are you—everything all right? You don't have to—for me—I don't care about that . . ."

Yet as she spoke her subtle motion began. He had only to hold her, her fragrance more musklike now, intermingled with the smell of the submarine: diesel fuel, emanations from the huge battery, the subtle but ineradicable essence of men working hard in close quarters for all the years since the submarine had been commissioned, mechanically ventilated but never knowing sunlight or the sweep of fresh sea breeze.

That was all mixed with her own precious smell, close and delightful, her flesh, her hair, her womanly excitement as she thrust inadvertently her soft fist against the tough steel hull.

"Hold me, honey, hold me, can you—are you—is—" her voice was lost in his throat her hair her hands all around him blowersound and footfall and slight distant knocking erased. It came upon him slowly, gathering from the periphery of his consciousness all the frantic images yearnings frustrations fears he felt it begin quite clearly outside himself, an explosion which began somewhere else began slowly and finally swept him up delivering him some time after she had subsided and lay awaiting his arrival, wifely, satisfied, complete.

"Honey," she said.

"Darling."

"There is somebody knocking."

"What?"

"Captain?"

They lay silently their breathing suspended.

"Captain—"

"Later! Go away, trying to sleep."

"Sorry, sir. Important message from the squadron office. Have to get your signature."

From the passageway a hand thrust in, holding a clipboard and a pencilstub. The ensign reached, took it, signed squinting in the dark, thrust it out.

"Okay," he snapped. "Shove off."

"The message, Captain. Here in this envelope."

"Leave it on the wardroom table."

"Aye, aye, sir."

They heard the footsteps moving off. The sailor had disarranged the curtain slightly and now a vagrant trace of light reflected against her face. Her face was flushed, tendrils of hair matted at her temples.

He held her against him, looking at the luminous dials and gauges in the captain's stateroom. They were under water right where they lay. The tug's propeller churned distantly beating at the water beside their heads.

"My God, Jimmie, I've never . . ."

"Shhh"—holding her—"shhhh . . ." suddenly aware of the curtain, the passageway, the other life out there, a certain bustle and purposeful movement, the sound of voices, everything seemed heightened, more insistent.

"Did you?" she said. "Are you all right? Did—"

"Sure."

"How can you be so—feel this. God." She put his hand to her temple. "I'm all wet."

"Your back, too," he said. "Right along here—"

"Be careful. Everywhere you touch me I just—could you just hold me for a while? Could we just stay here like this for a while?"

"Sure." He heard the sound of feet up on the main deck, deck lockers opening, closing; he lay listening to the waves lapping against the hull.

"I'm getting out of this crummy crew, off this lousy boat. I'm through. I've had enough of this. I'm going to ask for nuclear school right away. The hell with these damn things. Pig boats they used to call them. Well, they had it right. Don't try to talk me out of it."

"I'm tired of it too. I'm going with you."

"You mean it?"

"If you do."

The curtain jumped sideways. The light snapped on. It was the executive officer. They were so still and he was so intent pulling down the writing desk, pulling out one of the little drawers and looking for something that it was maybe five seconds before he saw them. When he did he just stood staring trying to understand what he was seeing, which was pretty much because they had laid down on the bunk still tightly made. There was not even a loose sheet now to draw over them. Then they all moved at once, the executive officer reaching for the ensign who in the same thrust that got his leg into his trousers kicked the executive officer in the chest.

"You sneaky bastard!" the executive officer cried. He grabbed the ensign's foot and pulled him off the bunk.

"You son of a bitch—" The ensign fell to the deck struggling with his trousers.

"Cover yourself up!" the executive officer shouted at Jacqueline.

"Why?" she said coolly sitting on the edge of the bunk getting her arms into her wraparound dress. "Nothing you haven't seen before," arching back her breasts catching the light from the passageway.

"In *flagrante delicto*," the ensign said from the deck, a flailing confusion of legs arms clothes. "You're an old hand at that—"

"—stinking little bastard!" the executive officer cried, kicking at the ensign and trying to pick him up to hit him at the same time. The ensign grabbed wildly and caught his trouserleg and the executive officer went sprawling through the door and across the passageway. A crowd had gathered, voluble and intent, though they seemed to be talking about something else. Sprague was there taking charge, shouting at the executive officer:

"Capm wants you on the bridge right now! We got to get underway immediately—Murphy, come on now, I'll take care of the kid—"

Sprague drew the curtain closed again and again they were alone in their cell, footsteps and voices on the other side in the other world.

Jacqueline was dressed now, seated on the bunkedge, putting on her shoes. They didn't say anything. She lighted a cigarette and he saw that her hand was shaking.

"It's his pride that's hurt more than anything," she said.

"I guess we better—"

Sprague came in. "You want to stay away from him for a while, Junior."

"He doesn't scare me."

"He sort of goes off his nut sometimes when he's real

mad. But after it's all over he is very sorry about what he done."

"So are the people he did it to," Jacqueline said.

"You got to get off, Jackie. We are going to sea right now."

"I'm not," the ensign said. "I'll just get my things and go along with her. So long, Sprague."

"You can't leave now, for Christ's sake!"

"You just watch me."

"We just got word they finally found him again. The admiral himself sent the word down. South end of area forty-five."

The ensign stared at him. "In the Op Areas? What's he doing there?"

"That's just it. Nobody knows. He might be in some kind of trouble."

"Is he submerged?"

"Yeah, but he's making a hell of a racket, like hammers and things. And pumps. Some destroyer picked him up by accident—"

"That's about where the Gulf Stream crosses the thousand-fathom curve."

"Yeah. He likes to work southwest of that, in the trench."

"If he's having propulsion trouble the Gulf Stream would set him toward us at maybe two or three knots—"

"Honey," Jacqueline said. "Come *on*—"

"—sort of like the sea was just delivering him up to us."

"Never get another chance like this," Sprague said.

"Jimmie—" Jacqueline said.

"Fish in a rain barrel," the ensign said, moving his finger past Sprague's face. "Bang! Like that."

Sprague looked at him. "Yeah. Well, something like that maybe. You better help me lay out the charts. We are getting the maneuvering watch set and as soon as we're underway we'll rig for dive and you'll have to check that. We're short-handed as usual. Take us damn near four hours to get out there full speed on the surface . . ."

They were walking aft along the passageway, stepping over the coaming into the control room, moving through it, talking. The mustang was standing by the hydraulic manifold studying a slide rule, giving orders to one of the chiefs to compensate the submarine for diving trim.

"Junior, how about checking these goddam numbers for me?"

"Sure, okay, Burt, in a minute. You go ahead and do your best and I'll check your work . . ."

The control room was crowded, sailors moving this way and that, the maneuvering watch was moving onto station, talkers were going forward and aft with their phones, their lines, a chief was taking reports on the intercom system on the status of the watch. Sailors were checking over the fathometer and the loran gear.

"You get in a battery charge last night?" the ensign said.

"Yeah. We lucked on that. Got a full can."

"Air banks full?"

"We'll have to jam some air on the way out."

They went up the ladder into the conning tower, another world, very cramped, but quiet and orderly, the helmsman checking out the engine order telegraph, the talker adjusting his headset.

In the after starboard corner Sprague's chart table had everything laid out like an operating room, dividers, pencils, slide rule, quartermaster's notebook all neatly placed on a folded damp towel to protect against the roll of the submarine at sea, pieces of tape neatly cut and tipped to the table's metal frame for quick access in changing charts, the charts themselves grouped, folded and stowed at the base of the chart table within easy reach, the channel chart taped down and the universal drafting machine in position.

The ensign looked at all that and looked through the charts checking them for order and sequence. As they ran off of one chart they would shift to the next and as they approached the target area they would want a large scale chart for that. The deck vibrated with the rumble of the main engines. From the bridge the captain's voice came down:

"Take in one! All back one third!"

"All back one third!" the helmsman cried, and jangled the annunciators. The submarine began to move, the whistle sounding its flat relentless blast.

"Holy Jesus!" the ensign cried, already moving, racing back down the ladder and through the control room and into the forward battery, looking for her in the captain's stateroom then the wardroom then the head then racing on through the forward torpedo room and up the ladder and through the hatch and onto the foredeck.

He saw her gliding by, waving. He waved hard, running forward until a sailor stopped him from running right off the bow. He shouted. He thought he heard her voice but he could not be sure. Then the submarine was backing into its turn, beginning its twist enginesroaring and she was going to the yellow Jaguar, getting in, driving off.

13

They went out of the channel at full speed. When they passed the sea buoy the captain called all the officers to the bridge. They were a pathetic bunch, the ensign thought: just the executive officer, the mustang, and himself besides the captain. Half the officer complement of a normal submarine. With all of them up here there were no officers at all below. He tried to feel alarmed, but knew instead a crazy swell of pride. The men knew their jobs. They could probably run the submarine with no officers at all if they had to. Regardless of their problems, they all wore dolphins.

With the wind distorting his words, the captain talked to them, shouting over the heavy noise of the engines and the rush and pull of the sea which the submarine took heavily on her bow, wallowing down, always down, as if hungry to dive. Heavy spray and some white water drifted back.

"They figure she is in some kind of trouble," the captain shouted, ducking behind the cowl when a sheet of water flew at them, all of them ducking too, huddled around him. "She was dead in the water for a while, about a hundred feet down. That's when that can found her. Just sort of stumbled onto her hanging there on a layer. But since that contact she got underway again. The best guess is that she has got some big trouble but has managed to patch it up whether for good or not nobody knows. The guess is she'll probably try to run for home."

"That means the Straits of Florida, then," the ensign said.

"Not necessarily," the executive officer said.

"No?" the captain said. "What else then?"

The executive officer managed to get a cigarette going in all that wind and now projected, even in the crouched wet huddle, his usual image of suave good looks, forceful and commanding.

"Well"—gesturing with the cigarette—"I mean we don't *know* he is having trouble. We don't *know* he is going to run for home. And we don't know he would head through the Straits if he did." The wind pulled the smoke from his mouth and nose.

"Yes," the ensign said. "He could go on down through the Yucatan Channel and around—"

"No. He'll go through the Straits."

"Damn it," the captain said. "You are just disagreeing with anything the kid says just to disagree."

"He is such a wise-ass little son of a bitch—"

"Never mind that now. We'll have to bank on his shooting for the Straits. It's a little closer for him so *if* he's in trouble and *if* he's heading home and *if* he chooses the closest way—lots of ifs—"

"And if the kid doesn't fuck us up—"

"*Will* you leave the kid alone now?"

"Orin—I got something to tell you about this smart-ass kid who he acts all the time like he's so goddam sweet and noble, but the first chance he—"

"Later. That's it for now. The destroyer that made the contact has left the area and all our submarines have been called in from the western op areas. So anything we find out there, that is the son of a bitch we are after."

"We better dive," the executive officer said.

"Not yet. I want to save the battery. You can all go below now. Junior, talk to you a minute."

"Orin—"

"Not right now, Murph."

They went below. The ensign stayed on the bridge. He enjoyed the tug and lash of the wind and seaspray. The captain didn't say anything for a while. They rode into the sea. The last trace of the magnificent red sunset faded and it began to grow dark. There was a little phosphorescence in the bow wave. The captain lighted a thin cigar.

"Kid, want you to know you been doing pretty good in your progress toward Qualification. Been keeping an eye on you. All you got left to do is fire your torpedo underway and you'll get your dolphins. That's pretty rare for a youngster's never been to sub school."

"When can we work in the torpedo firing?"

The captain shrugged. "You know how things are with us. Your daddy had to bootleg us the warshots we have on board. One fourteen and an acoustic—"

"We ought to have more than that."

"He says that gives us a spare." They rode in silence for some more and then the captain said, "We ought to have a lot more of a lot of things. But your daddy doesn't want to get the G.A.O. stirred up about us. Most of what we've got isn't listed anyplace any more. Certainly not the warshots. God knows what he had to do to get them but he got them."

"You know my father pretty well."

The captain looked at him. "If it hadn't been for him I never would have been commissioned. Murphy either."

He looked away, studying the dancing lights in the bow wave. "I was—we were in sort of a scrape at the Academy —I thought you knew about this—and—"

"And the superintendent of the Academy hushed it up. A captain."

"That's right. And the captain was your dad."

It was quite dark now. In the distance the lights of civilian ships traced their stately patterns along the steamerlanes.

"I'd like you to be diving officer when we submerge. You're better at that than Burt, now. Some guys got a natural feel for it, some guys never quite seem to get the hang of it. Burt's okay, but you got the touch, kid."

"Captain!"

It was the mustang, standing on the conning tower ladder, just his head visible as if someone had laid it on the deck.

"You all ready to dive, Burt?"

"No, sir. Not right yet. We got more trouble with that engine exhaust valve than we thought. It's in the linkage."

"Who you got on it?"

"Working on it myself. The inboard valve looks weak too."

"Can I dive?"

"I wouldn't if I was you."

"But can I if I have to?"

"Only if it's an emergency."

"Okay. Thanks, Burt. Get on back and supervise the work. You're an officer now. Put one of the men on it."

When he had gone the captain said, "Jesus, just our being out here is an emergency. But I'll put off diving. I was going to dive about here."

"My father," the ensign said. "My dad was superintendent—when you—so he must have—"

"I think we are okay on the surface for a while anyway. A submarine on the surface looks like a fishing boat or almost anything in the dark. Still, I'll feel better when we can dive."

He leaned on the talk button on the bridge transmitter.

"Control! Tell Mr. Murphy to bear a hand with the work on negative vent."

Still hunched over the speaker, he looked around at the ensign as the acknowledgment crackled back. "That won't help anything, but it makes me feel better. One of the worst skippers I ever knew taught me that principle: when there is nothing to be done, relieve your anxiety by shouting at somebody about it. I have followed it scrupulously since. His theory was that ulcers are assigned on a quota system to groups of people, and as long as you make sure the people around you have theirs, you are safe. Something about the law of averages."

"He must have been some captain," the ensign said.

"You met him the other day. Spunky Waters."

"I—I met him once before that. In the channel."

"Yeah. That chicken of the sea crap."

"Did Mr. Murphy tell you about that?"

"No. Spunky did. I'm afraid the *Devilfish* gave Spunky some bad memories for his last days in the submarine force."

"You mean Commander Waters is out of the Navy?"

"No, no. Just the boats. He got orders to a tin can. Skipper of a destroyer now, gave him the old *Everly*. Still operates out of Key West. See how the other half lives. Wonder how long it will take him to give an entire destroyer wardroom an ulcer. Spunky took over the *Everly* this morning."

"He must have been mad at Mr. Murphy for that chicken of the sea business."

"Oh, they have hated each other's guts cordially for some years. Though I must say Spunky was willing to give up the feud long ago. He's married now. Kids."

"What's that have to do with it?"

The captain looked around at him. "Jackie."

The ensign didn't say anything.

"Murph has had what you might call a sort of protective interest in my wife for some time. Long and complicated story. For a while there she seemed interested in Spunky, so Murph told him to stay the hell away and Spunky told him to go to hell and one thing just sort of led to another . . ."

My wife, the ensign thought wildly. So they are—*Say, are you two really married after all?* he tried to imagine himself saying, but could not. Immobile, his glasses to his eyes studying the horizon but not seeing much, he waited for the captain to continue, but the captain had fallen silent.

"That must be sort of complicated," the ensign said finally. "Having a fellow like Mr. Murphy looking out for your wife . . ."

The bridge speaker crackled. It was the executive officer. "Negative vent looks okay now. Now it's the flood I'm worried about."

"Aye," the captain said. "Keep on it." He released the button. "You and Jackie," he said. "I know about that."

The ensign studied the horizon hard.

"Thing I care about is that she's happy," the captain said. "That Murphy is bad news. Always has been. All he is, is he's handsome. Handsome Harold they called him at the Academy. Manners, all that. Underneath a real son of a bitch."

"Well, but does she—"

"No!" the captain looked abruptly over. "And she never

did. Sorry for him is all. That's all it ever was. But of course he is the biggest ladies' man the world has ever known, so naturally he never could accept that."

"Captain!" It was Sprague in the conning tower, shouting up the hatch. "Radar contact two oh double oh, three four zero!"

"Son of a bitch!" the captain said. "Turn off that radar. Who told you to turn that on?"

"Mr. Murphy, sir."

To the ensign he said, "They'll d.f. us, if they haven't already." He leaned over the hatch, speaking quietly. "All stop. Call Mr. Foster in the forward engine room and tell him to knock off work on those exhaust valves. I want absolute silence. Is the chief sonarman in the conning tower?"

"Right here, Captain."

"Chekenian, I want you to listen to this guy."

"Aye, sir."

Divested of power the submarine coasted ghostlike through the dark water, tiny flicks of phosphorescence speckling the bow wave.

"He is making a good bit of noise, Captain."

"What's it sound like?"

"Hammering mostly. Some machinery sounds. Not engines. Pumps maybe, something like that."

"He must be in trouble all right," the captain said. "Probably why he is on the surface."

"Wouldn't this be a good time to shoot him, then?" the ensign said. He said it very calmly. Only after he spoke did the words begin to have meaning and gather in his stomach.

"Not until I can dive."

"But if he is having trouble maybe he can't dive."

"I'd sure like to know." He called down the hatch, "What's his range now?"

"We secured the radar, Captain."

"Damn it!" He leaned to the talk switch. "Maneuvering, answer bells on the battery." And down the hatch he called, "All ahead one third. Light off the radar and keep it going."

The submarine began to pick up speed.

"Steer three four zero," the captain said.

"That's right toward him," the ensign said. He was finally beginning to realize what they were actually out here to do.

"Give him a little something to think about," the captain said. "If he can dive, he'll dive."

"Maybe he can't see us."

"I'm sure he's seen us or heard us by now."

The executive officer's voice was the first indication he was standing behind them on the bridge.

"Orin, what the hell are you doing?"

"Just closing him a touch."

"We have taken a lot of water in the engine room bilges. You can't dive till they pump it out."

"I don't want the pump on the line yet. See what he does, first."

"Torpedo us. That's what he'll do."

"My guess is no."

"I hope you're right."

"If he *can* dive he *will* dive as we close him."

"Well, what good will that do? *We* can't dive."

"Look, we can't put a torpedo in him on the surface any more than he can put one in us. That's a shipping lane right out there." The captain pointed toward the parade of stately lights passing some miles away: the tall masthead lights, the range lights, an occasional dim red or green very low to the water, a cruise ship way in the distance moving in its own tight cluster of white light.

"Nobody wants any surface torpedo action. His orders are to get our nukes and get them submerged. We're not a nuke and we're not submerged. That's our protection."

"We know that. You sure he knows that?"

"He knows. They don't send idiots out here for the kind of work he's been doing."

"Well, if you make him dive he'll just get away and we'll have to find him all over again."

"We'll shoot him on the way down. As soon as he has negative buoyancy. A diving submarine is the most vulnerable vessel there is, nuke or not."

"By God, it just might work!" The executive officer's voice sounded excited for the first time. "He couldn't see us or hear us. He'd just be counting on speed—"

"—which he wouldn't have time to get cranked on yet. We'll put one in him at about fifty feet—"

"—before he even has a chance to blow negative!"

"That's the idea."

"He'll sink like a rock!"

"If we do it right. *Range!*"

"One five double oh!" Sprague shouted up at once.

"What do you—*there he is!*" The captain had for some time been looking through his binoculars toward the bearing of the contact. Now the executive officer and the ensign studied the same stretch of dark horizon, the ensign, expecting to find a discernible submarine superstructure, perhaps with a little Russian flag flying, had finally to settle for the small amorphous lump he finally managed to find, a tiny spot of blackness against the infinite dark, ominous in its near invisibility. Were there *men* attached to that thing? Living breathing men, walking, talking, working, bunks, machinery, engines, torpedoes?

"What do you figure his angle on the bow is?" the captain said.

"Damn hard to tell," the executive officer said. "Hard to see much."

"What's it matter?" the ensign said. "He's dead in the water."

"If he is going to dive he'll have to get underway as he goes down. We'll have to know where he is when our torpedo gets there."

"It's either starboard thirty or port one-fifty. I can't tell which is the bow and which is the stern."

"Let's make it starboard thirty. You better crank that in."

"I better stay up on the bridge, Orin. Junior can do it."

"I want him on the dive."

"Burt can take the dive. Kid, you're checked out on the TDC. Nothing to this one. Set target speed zero, angle on the bow starboard thirty and if he gets underway we'll tell you and you put in speed, oh, say about ten knots. We'll use the acoustic fish. All we have to do is get it near his screws, and it will home on the noise. All there is to it."

"But couldn't I stay—"

"Get below," the executive officer snapped. "On the double."

The ensign jumped down the ladder and went to the TDC.

"Gimme a range," he said.

"One two double oh."

The ensign pressed the talk button on the mike to the bridge. "Range one two double oh, Captain. Setting gyros for zero. Torpedo run same as range—"

"Very well, Junior. Stand by."

"Captain, we are all ready except that the outer door is still shut."

"Get it open."

The ensign called the forward torpedo room. "Open the outer door on tube number one. Stand by one."

Distantly he heard the outer door open.

The mustang, dripping wet, was standing on the ladder, jutting up through the conning tower deck. "Kid, tell the captain we are losing ground in the engine room. The bilges are flooded and more is leaking in. We got to start the drain pump."

"How bad is it?"

"We're okay for a while. Long as we don't dive. Tell him I want permission to start the pump now."

The mustang was holding a mug of steaming coffee as he delivered his message. He went below. The ensign pressed the talk button on the 7 m.c. and relayed his report.

When there was no response he said it all again. Then he went to the ladder and climbed up to the bridge. He emerged to find the captain and the executive officer staring into a flashing white light coming not from the target bearing but from abaft the starboard beam.

"What's that?" the ensign said.

"Get the hell below," the executive officer said.

"You read flashing light?" the captain said.

"Sure."

"Get back on the TDC," the executive officer said.

"What's this guy saying?" the captain said. "We're both a little rusty."

"Who is it?" the ensign said.

"Maybe if you'd read the light we'd be able to tell you," the captain said.

"He's sending a six-letter group over and over—"

"I can see that much," the executive officer said. "You don't have to stand one in your class to figure that much out."

"What's it say?" the captain said.

"Foxtrot—Item—George—Able—Roger—Oboe. That's it. Now he's sending it all over again."

"What the hell do you suppose it means?"

"Me?" the ensign said. "I don't have any idea."

"Not some kind of code or something we're supposed to know about?"

"How would I know?"

"You're the assistant navigator and operations officer," the executive officer said. "It's your job to know these things."

"Nothing in the mail the last few days."

"Before that?" the captain said.

"Then either. I would have remembered."

They all stood there, not moving, the letters spelled out rapidly across the water.

"It must be a commie signal of some sort," the executive officer said.

"But he's aiming the light right at us," the captain said. "I think it's a destroyer."

"Probably one of their fishing trawlers," the executive officer said. "They're all over the place."

"I wish to hell I knew what it meant," the captain said.

"Mr. Foster wants us to put the pump on the forward engine room, Captain. He says—"

"Probably telling the sub he is here to escort him home," the executive officer said.

"I don't like the smell of this," the captain said. "The admiral didn't say anything about anything like this. A surface ship. We better disengage."

"Because of a lousy fishing trawler?" the executive officer said.

"I don't know what that signal means."

"They wouldn't send a tin can out to help a submarine," the executive officer said. "Would they?"

"They'd probably send whatever they had steaming around in the Gulf or the Caribbean or the Straits that was closest. They got a lot of destroyers in these waters. They got a lot of everything."

"He just keeps sending F-I-G-A-R-O over and over," the ensign said.

"Chekenian," the captain said down the hatch. "I am going to pull away a few hundred yards. If he gets underway to follow me, see if you can tell me what kind of ship it is. About one zero zero relative. All ahead one third, left full rudder."

He steadied up heading away, then ran for a while, turned back toward and stopped.

"He is underway all right, Captain," Chekenian called up the hatch. "It's a can."

"You sure?"

"Sounds like one for sure. Twin screws, and lighter than their fishing trawlers, faster beats. I never really heard a commie destroyer, but it sounds a lot like ours and that's what ours sound like all right."

"Could it be one of ours?" the ensign said.

"No," the executive officer said. "All our ships are clear of these waters."

"We can't out run him," the captain said. There was a little strain in his voice now.

"We better put a fish in him," the executive officer said.

"No," the captain said. "We're not supposed to do that."

"He's a target of opportunity," the executive officer said.

"Whatever he was sending, he quit sending it," the ensign said. He was studying the indistinct silhouette, blinking his eyes against the afterglow of the light, when his field of vision turned yelloworange, defining instantaneously a destroyerlike image, incredibly bright, then gone as the shockwave came enveloped in gunroar.

14

The executive officer was standing on the step at the right side of the bridge when the shell struck. He simply broke in half. One minute he was standing there saying something and the next his upper body disappeared in a rolling ball of fire and sound.

The captain was on the port bridge step and took some of the blast in his chest but mostly his face, his binoculars driven back hard into his eyes. He was down on the deck on his side, his hands frozen to the binoculars which his arms still held to his face.

"Captain!" the ensign cried, down on his knees beside him. "Captain!" pulling at his shoulders. The binoculars were shattered, he held only the shells which seemed melded to some spongy amalgam of tissue, flesh blood bone.

Sprague was beside him. "Junior—what the hell hap—"

"Dive! Take her down!"

"You're wounded. Your arm—"

"Never mind. Leave me here. Take her down anyway! Dive, damn it! *That's an order—*"

"Well, I ain't going to leave the captain up here."

Sprague and the ensign (the ensign was trembling and stuttering, it was mostly Sprague) got the captain shoved down the hatch to waiting hands.

"What about—that?" Sprague said, gesturing toward

the obscenity at the starboard side, the remnants of the executive officer.

The ensign felt nausea gather, bit down hard against it. "Leave it."

The diving alarm never got sounded. The chief of the watch in control room pulled the vents as soon as Sprague slammed the hatch and shouted, "Okay, I got 'em!" and the helmsman rang up full speed ahead.

"Get her down fast!" the ensign shouted down the lower hatch at the planesmen. "Get some angle on her!"

"Heavy aft!" the stern planesman shouted back. "Hard to get a down angle!"

"I'll give you speed. All ahead emergency!"

The helmsman had it rung up before the ensign finished saying it.

"Sprague, have the forward room shut number one tube door."

"I just checked. They already shut it."

The captain lay tossed on the conning tower deck like a broken toy. Sprague went to him and rolled him over this way. The ensign saw the face and his stomach lurched and he began to gag, looking away. He found himself looking at the bald head of the mustang coming up the ladder.

"Burt! I'd like you to take the dive. We—"

"You better get this thing back up on the surface right now," the mustang said. "Or you never will. What the hell do you think you're doing? You didn't even sound the diving alarm. We got caught with the inboard valve open and it's the outboard one that's broke."

"We've got more to worry about than a little water."

"More'n a *little* water you dumb shit. Where the hell is the captain?"

The ensign told him what had happened.

"So now I suppose you think you are the captain—" the mustang said.

"No. You are. You're senior—"

"Fuck it!" the mustang said. He tore the tarnished silver bars from his collarpoints and tossed them on the conning tower deck. "I never did like it nohow. All that la-de-dah crap up forward. Never did belong there. Now see the mess you Academy apes has got us in. Well, you get us out. I don't care one way or the other. I'll be back in the engine room, seeing what I can do for you," he said, going down. "You're still a dumb shit."

"For you too!" the ensign shouted after him.

"Fuck it," the mustang said. "It's all a bunch of cheese, no matter how you slice it."

"How is your arm, Captain?" Sprague said.

The ensign whirled around. "His arm? My God, his arm is the least of his—"

"Yours, I mean. You're bleeding."

Command at sea is a magical thing. It stanches the blood and relieves the pain. All the sailors in the conning tower were standing looking at him. His right arm, shoulder, and side, torn and bleeding, were in a condition which in another circumstance and an earlier time would have sent him to the hospital for weeks. Now he knew he was hurt by looking at himself, but that was all. If anything, the sight strangely exhilarated him. He felt blooded, tested, a triumphant veteran of holocaust.

He looked at the tarnished silver bars where they lay on the deck, picked them up, and put them in his pocket.

"All stop!" he snapped. "Sprague, have the drain pump put on the forward engine-room bilges at once."

"Aye aye," Sprague said and got on the phone.

Chekenian strained intently to his sonar, earphones big against his immobile head. He was as sweaty and tired as the rest, yet his neat blue uniform and white chief's hat gave the forward starboard corner of the conning tower a peculiarly decorous air.

"Here is the submarine," he said, calling out the bearing. "Sounds like she is getting underway. And here is the destroyer. He's making knots . . . closing us . . ."

"He's making a run!" Sprague said. They could hear him right through the hull now, an express train overhead coming this way. They all stood looking up. From the depth gauge the ensign could see they were under water, were going down nicely. He leaned over the lower hatch.

"Blow negative!"

"Blow negative, aye!" the chief shouted, and instantly the high pressure air hit the tank.

"All ahead one third," the ensign said.

"He is going to drop," Sprague said. "Better—"

"No," the ensign said. "He won't. What we have to worry about now is did that shell loosen any fittings. The main hatch seems okay. I think it hit low, base of the fairwater, blew off some of the superstructure, but as long as the pressure hull isn't leaking we're okay."

"What makes you think he won't drop?" Sprague said. They could hear the screws churning the water frantically.

"He is just hurrying over to see what happened to us. He's worried."

"About what?"

"That was just a warning shot across our bow."

"Our *bow?*"

"He missed. He was just supposed to warn us off, *supposed* to be across our bow, now he is worried and coming over to see what happened. You see at night on the surface a submarine is quite difficult to see."

Command is heady in other ways too. Sprague just

stared at him. The ensign picked up the phone and called the forward engine room. "Foster? How is—"

"Foster ain't here," the voice said. "Who's this?"

"This is the, uh, Mr. Hillerby. How are you doing back there?"

"Oh. You'll be pretty heavy, Captain, but we got the flooding controlled now. We're holding okay with just the inboard valve. Foster fixed it hisself."

"Put him on."

"He's up in the galley."

"We got trouble there too?"

"Naw, he's getting a cup of joe."

The ensign felt the sound coming before he really heard it but he didn't have any idea what it was. An earthquake, was his first thought. The deck lifted straight up then dropped leaving him for an instant suspended in the air. When he landed the deck was no longer level but slanting sickly to one side and down.

It came again, a hard metallic whing*whang* embedded in a shock wave profound and endless. The submarine shuddered, lifted, tilted, dropped, angling up then down even more sharply.

Sprague was crumpled in the rear of the conning tower, coffee all over him and ashes from a buttkit that had fallen. He got up on one elbow, shaking his head.

"You sure about that, Captain? That he ain't going to drop on us?"

Chekenian had been caught by surprise with his volume up and his headphones on. He was up and pirouetting in an anguished circle, his head between his hands, blood trickling thinly from one ear and down his cheek. From Orin Feldman's crumpled form came a low moan.

"Get the captain below," the ensign said.

"What?" Sprague said. "You what?"

"Feldman. Get him out of here. Take him below."

They were already lifting him. He seemed to be conscious going down the ladder, grasping the handrails himself.

"Take him to his stateroom," the ensign shouted. "Get him in his bunk. See what you can do for him." *Maybe some brandy,* he thought to add, but didn't. He couldn't remember about his mouth.

Thinking about Feldman, he managed to be taken by surprise again by the next explosion. The submarine bucked furiously, the hull vibrating with an eerie hum, and the lights went out. He clawed his way to the forward end of the conning tower and found the microphone by feel and hung on as he shouted, "Shut all watertight doors and bulkhead flappers! Rig for depth charge attack!"

"We rigged after the first drop, Captain!" somebody shouted up from control room, not sarcastic, just reporting.

The ensign realized the air conditioning had been off for some time now, the inside of the conning tower was like a steam bath. It was pitch black. Only the luminous dials of the instruments were visible.

Sprague's battered face appeared, floating in the dark, a bodiless specter illuminated from below. He had turned on a flashlight.

"Turn on the battle lamps," the ensign said.

"Been checking 'em. Batteries is missing from some, bulbs from another, and two is just plain gone. The guys like 'em for various things . . ."

From the dark some sailor's voice said, "Git out your little notebook, Junior, and put 'em on report—" the phrase accompanied by the moving flashlight which, from the sound, hit the speaker in the mouth.

"Stow that shit, sailor. Show the captain some respect."

"Well, he ain't—"

"He's all we got," Sprague said. "He'll do."

"Make your depth three hundred feet!" the ensign shouted down the hatch. He spoke into brilliant light-glare. Somebody was standing on the ladder holding a battle lantern pointed up. "Found this, Captain. Thought you might—"

"Sprague, here's a lantern. Rig it up somewhere."

"Captain!" the stern planesman called. "We're already passing three hundred and fifty feet and going down."

Sprague rigged the battle lantern in a bracket on the bulkhead and stood looming squat and solid in the side-glow. The ensign went to him and said quietly,

"What's our collapse depth?"

"Never mind that."

"Four hundred, isn't it?"

"We'll know in a minute."

Sprague just stood there noticeably paler in the light from the battle lantern. The ensign jumped down the hatch, guiding his fall by the handrails, and landed behind the planesmen, two young sailors, one of them the one with the scar and the bad eye. They were frozen, chiaroscuro figures in the flat battle-lanternlight, watching the needle in the depth gauge move steadily around toward four hundred feet.

The bowplanes were on hard rise but the stern planesman had his planes reversed, chasing the vanished bubble, and was on hard dive. The ensign hit him on the shoulder.

"Watch your bubble! Go the other way! *Come on, goddam it!*"

The boy looked around helplessly, his face fearstruck the good eye glazed. No wisecracks now, no smart answers. The ensign put his hands on the huge green wheel and turned it in short jabs, hitting the hydraulic motors rhythmically, until the bubble reappeared in the glass. The sickening down angle began to ease.

"There she is," the ensign said. "Now watch it, no, no, this way—that's it. Careful. Easy does it—see? Okay, you got it now. It's all yours. You can handle it. Everybody gets mixed up now and then. Okay?"

"Yes, sir. Thank you, sir."

"I want an up bubble now, pretty big one. Make it ten up. I'll give you flank speed to drive her up."

"Ten up, aye, aye, Captain." Attentively the stern planesman nursed the big wheel, coaxing the bubble over.

"Bowplanes, I want full rise, but you are in the stops. Take a little of that off so you don't jam the planes. *All ahead flank!*" The annunciator bells jangled in the conning tower. He clapped them both on their shoulders. "We don't have any diving officer, but I'll coach you from the conning tower. If you get into any trouble just sing out."

"I'll watch 'em too, Captain," the grizzled old chief of the watch said from the control manifold. He had picked up his coffeecup. "I shoulda been watching 'em more careful, but when we got down that deep I guess I kind of—"

"It's okay, Chief. Don't worry. Happens to us all."

They were moving up nicely now, passing three hundred feet, two seventy-five, two fifty. The ensign climbed back up the ladder.

"All ahead one third. I want to save the battery. No telling how long we'll be down."

He looked at Chekenian who was back at the sonar gear, grimly adjusting the set. "How are your ears, Chief?"

"What?"

"Can you hear anything?"

"What? Bastards busted an eardrum. Other one is okay, I think. Getting better."

"Sprague, get his relief up here."

"His relief didn't make it aboard," Sprague said. "I wonder why the hell that guy didn't drop any more? He sounded like he meant business."

"I wish I knew." Down the hatch he said, "Make your depth one five oh."

"One five oh, aye."

"Can you hold that with this speed?"

"Yes sir, if we keep the up bubble."

"Okay." He went to Chekenian and leaned down close to his ear. "Chief—can you hear anything?"

"What? I can hear better in the phones than I can without! That submarine is underway now for sure!"

"Keep at it."

"His screws has speeded up. Bearing is steady!"

The lights came on. That would be the mustang's work. *Bless that competent s.o.b.*, the ensign thought. *Now I hope he gets back on those engine exhaust valves. I am going to recommend him for the Navy Cross.*

"You think he knows where we are?" the ensign said.

"We'll soon find out," Sprague said. The ensign went back to where Sprague stood by the chart table. He had the DRT bug going and had been keeping his plots up to date with whatever information was available.

"I lost the bug when we lost the lighting load, but I advanced it by hand and I think it's pretty close."

"If you did it, I know damn well it's close."

"Thanks, Skipper." Something like a crack appeared in Sprague's rockface and the ensign realized he was smiling. "Here's where we are. And here's where I figure that submarine is. Somewhere on this bearing anyway."

"What's he up to?"

"I figure he is running for the Straits okay. We're all that's between him and it. Once he gets through there he's

got a million places to hide. We'd never be able to find
him or do anything about it if we could. He can lie there
and pick off the next new nuke any damn time he pleases,
and get away with it again."

"This submarine is coming in damn fast!" Chekenian
called. He shouted everything at the top of his voice now.

The ensign went to the TDC and cranked in target
course as the reciprocal of target bearing.

"Bearing is steady!" Chekenian shouted. "We are on a
collision course with the submarine!"

"That's what he is doing all right," the ensign said.
"Running for the Straits. Can you estimate his speed?"

Chekenian sat in his dark blue uniform with red hashmarks covering the forearm looking at his stopwatch and
counting against it with his finger. He looked like a distinguished surgeon called in on a desperate case.

"Damn fast!" he shouted. "I'd give him thirty-five, forty
knots!"

"That's not possible," Sprague said.

"I'll give him twenty-five," the ensign said. He cranked
the little wheel to get it into the TDC.

"Faster than that!" Chekenian shouted.

"We've got a good bearing," the ensign said. "Let's try
for a sonar range."

"He might hear us," Sprague said.

The chief called up the hatch, "Awful heavy aft, Captain. Beginning to lose depth control again."

"I'll take the chance," the ensign said. "Get me a
range."

"Single ping," Sprague said.

"As many goddam pings as you need!" the ensign said.

"Sorry, Skipper," Sprague said. "During the war we—"

"This is a different war."

"Yeah. In this one we're the enemy—"

Chekenian had trained carefully and was keying his gear. They heard the pings going out into the water. Then they heard them find the target and make their bounce-back. Sprague whistled. "That is some doppler."

"Four oh double oh!" Chekenian shouted.

The ensign set it into the TDC. "Okay," he said. "That checks. We been heading away all this time and he probably went the other way when he got underway and dived."

"Bearing is still steady!" Chekenian shouted.

"Okay," the ensign said. He moved from the TDC to the chart table. He tried to keep his voice steady. It kept rising and he had to keep clearing his throat.

"Get me another sonar range," he said. "Then we'll know."

He saw the mustang's head lying on the deck, round and shiny. He was standing on the ladder, his head in the hatch.

"Junior—" he said.

"Captain," Sprague said.

"—the forward engine room—"

"Later," the ensign said.

"This is later now. We can't control the flooding no more. The sea valve carried away and now the inboard has gone too. She's just pouring in back there."

"Two five double oh!" Chekenian cried, punching his stopwatch. Sprague punched his too.

"Damn near a mile," Sprague said. "In just a little over a minute."

"Stick a cork in it," the ensign said. The mustang just looked at him. Sprague was working out the problem on the nautical slide rule. He stared at the slide rule. "Fifty knots!"

"Fifty knots?" the mustang's head said from the deck.

"It's your new Navy and you're bloody well welcome to it." His head disappeared. They heard him shouting something down below, laughing, and the phrase *fifty knots* drifted up.

Chekenian had been working it out longhand. "Fifty knots!" he announced.

The ensign went to the TDC and cranked target speed up to fifty knots. They were all looking at him. The ensign's face had changed. The youthful brightness was still there but now it was overlaid with that kind of desperation which can under the right circumstances become courage, or in the wrong ones, panic. He felt the two alternating, surging and pulling within him. He fought off the urge to crawl whimpering under the chart table, his hands over his head.

Sprague was shouting almost as loud as Chekenian now. "At that speed he'll run right into us in less than a minute now!"

"Right full rudder!" the ensign said. "Steer zero eight zero. Tell the tubes forward to stand by. I don't know enough to trust myself for a down the throat shot. It's too hard. I'll get off his track and shoot him as he goes by with as close to a ninety-degree torpedo-track angle as I can. That's the best kind of shot. You can't beat that kind of shot. All the aces during the war, they always tried for a ninety track angle when they could, the books all say that's best, you see with a ninety track you have all the advantages of—"

"Okay, Skipper," Sprague said, his voice firm and calm. "Whatever you decide. If you don't do it, it ain't gonna get done."

"What if I miss him?"

"You ain't going to miss."

The ensign went to the TDC and stood turning the

dials doing two men's jobs setting it all in, making his calculations. For a few isolated seconds he lost himself in the
sheer cold beauty of the problem everything neat orderly
quiet sine cosine tangent own ship target ship a sanitary
mathematical system with interlocking and interdepend-
ent parts controlled by knurled knobs automatic input and
elegant trigonometric equations as constant as time and
inviolable as the progress of the stars and the moon.

15

The phone whirped and Sprague took the report. "It's the forward engine room. They think we may have a ruptured fuel tank. We're losing fuel."

"That's probably why he stopped depth-charging us," the ensign said. "He saw the oil slick and figured he'd sunk us."

"Yeah," Sprague said. "It must be light up there by now."

"Well, that gives us a little time. How long do you think this thing will hold together?"

"Long enough," Sprague said. "But no longer."

"What?" Chekenian said.

"Open the outer door on tube number one," the ensign said. "Tell tubes forward to stand by one." He was studying the set up on the TDC. The TDC was made for periscope work, but he was doing pretty well. All he had to do was get within a thousand yards. "Get me another range and bearing."

Chekenian keyed his gear and they heard the sound impulse go out and return. He reported his findings at full bellow, his voice going raw and hoarse now. They made their calculations.

"Speed checks!" Sprague said.

"Course checks," the ensign said. "We have a firing solution. We'll shoot from the information generating in the TDC when distance to the track is exactly eight hundred yards."

He watched his dials and indicators. A feeling of immense power and control came over him. It was very quiet. In the silence he heard the groan of the bowplane motor, the clank and sigh of the hydraulic accumulator. He watched Sprague standing by the firing key.

"Stand by!" he said. "Distance to the track . . . twelve hundred . . . a thousand . . . eight—*fire!*"

Sprague hit the key.

"Lost his screw noises!" Chekenian shouted.

"You mean we hit him?"

"No. I didn't hear no explosion. He's just stopped his engines."

"How is our fish doing?"

"What?"

"Our fish. How—"

"Hot, straight, and normal."

"Jesus," Sprague said. "Them acoustic fish can't find him if he ain't making any noise. You should of used the Mark 14. Only two fish to choose from and you choose the wrong one. Jesus anyway."

"He must have heard the door open," the ensign said. "He's worried about acoustic fish, so he has turned everything off."

"So goddam close and then to miss him," Sprague said. "You shouldn't have shot so soon. You should have waited."

"Losing depth control!" the chief shouted up the hatch. "Getting very heavy amidships too now."

"It's the engine room," Sprague said.

"Must be something more. Something forward of that. Pump room maybe—"

The chief was on the ladder again. "We're taking water in the pump room through negative vent!"

"You got your flood shut?"

"Of course we got the goddam flood shut!"

"Well, then you can't be flooding!"

The chief just looked at him. "Well, she checks shut on the Christmas tree."

"Don't just stand there. Find the trouble and fix it."

"We got to start the drain pump."

"No pumping yet." He turned to Sprague. "He can't just stop dead in the water. At that speed he'd have terrific way on. What the hell would he do? If he's scared of us he'd probably turn hard one way or the other. And probably surface . . ."

The ensign rushed back to the chart in the after starboard corner and studied the DRT track. "We are going to have to estimate his turning circle and his amount of advance and transfer. And guess at which way he turned."

"Why?" Sprague said. "We already missed him."

"We have the Mark 14 steam fish in tube number two. The solution is still generating in the TDC."

"But he stopped."

"Just his engines. *He* didn't stop. He's still somewhere. All we have to do is figure out where and correct the TDC. Tell the forward room to stand-by tube two and keep their gyros matched on the Mickey Mouse."

When Sprague got off the phone, the ensign said, "Come on. We'll draw it."

"Draw what?"

The ensign hit Chekenian on the shoulder and got him up and moving aft, shouting in his good ear, "Come back here to the chart table, Chief! Need you for a minute!"

They all hunched over the chart table, sweat running from their foreheads chins throats, their hands wet and sticky with it; the paper was wet and hard to draw on with the hard fine pencils.

"Here is his vector," the ensign said. "At that course and speed let's figure a turn away with full rudder. He might have turned toward and he might not have turned at all, so it's just a guess, but I think it's what he should have done. Now I want you to fair in what the curve would look like. Best you can." He had to repeat a lot of that for Chekenian.

Sprague in his dungarees and T shirt and Chekenian in his dress blues drenched through with sweat began to draw the curve. It was partly guesswork, but not completely. Chekenian knew some of the characteristics of the enemy submarine and Sprague knew submerged turning circles for various classes of vessel at certain speeds.

"I never drew no fifty-knot curve before," Sprague said.

"Okay," Chekenian said.

"Something like that," Sprague said.

"All right," the ensign said. He stepped back to the TDC. He felt preternaturally confident and knew a sense of exhilaration larger than danger though danger was its very core. "Now read me off his new course and estimate the speed by the time he's been without power."

Sprague could do that pretty accurately. He had a deceleration curve for own ship tacked neatly over his chart table. He made his extrapolations, made his guess, gave the ensign the estimated new course and speed. The ensign cranked it into the TDC.

"Stand by for a surface approach," the ensign said. "Have the forward room set depth ten, speed high."

"Wait a minute," Sprague said. "How do you know he'll surface?"

"How do we know anything?" the ensign said. "We

don't. We just have to make some educated guesses and take our chances."

Sprague started to argue some more but the ensign shouted, "All stop! Chief, take a listen all around—I said, *listen all around now*, dammit!"

They stood immobile, staring at Chekenian's blue back as the deck began to tilt to an up angle and boat began to slip backward to greater depth. Just as the ensign was about to put on an ahead bell, Chekenian shouted,

"She blowing! She's blowing main ballast!"

"Periscope depth!" the ensign called. "Smartly now!"

"Speed!" the chief called up the hatch.

"All ahead two thirds!"

"More than that! We're slipping backwards still!"

"All ahead emergency!" He was sweating so heavily it got in his eyes and blurred his vision, a steady moist film.

"That's holding us, but it don't look like we're going to get up with it."

"Jesus, Chief. It's all we've got."

"Light fast screws!" Chekenian cried. "*Torpedo!*"

"What bearing?"

"Coming from our own firing bearing—it sounds like ours."

"That goddam acoustic fish!" Sprague said.

"It's doubling back toward us," Chekenian said. He didn't shout. He sounded awed, his voice cracking.

"It's homing on our own screws now," Sprague said. "Better ring up all stop."

The helmsman had his hand on the annunciators.

"No!" the ensign called. "We'll lose our depth. We'll lose our shot at him."

"Well, if we blow ourselves up we'll lose it anyway," Sprague said.

"How far away is it?" the ensign said. "The fish."

"I don't know," Chekenian said.

"Well, ping on it!"

"What?"

"*Ping—*"

"On the torpedo?"

"You can do it. Go ahead. Hurry. I want to know how much time I've got."

Then he shouted down the hatch:

"Put a bubble in safety. Just enough to help us up. Don't lose depth control."

They felt the short, hard jolt of air. The ensign watched the depth gauge. The submarine began to lift faster.

"She's so little it's hard to read the echo," Chekenian said. "I figure maybe five hunnert yards."

"We'll just out run the damn thing. All ahead emergency!"

"Already are all ahead emergency!" the helmsman said.

"You can't out run one of them torpedoes," Sprague said. "They go—"

"I know how fast they go! All we have to do is get to the surface long enough to get a final shooting bearing on that bastard. Just one quick look at him. That's all."

They all stood staring at him, even the helmsman was looking around over his shoulder. Nobody said anything.

"Well, that's what we're here for, isn't it?"

They all held on as the deck slanted up. The air in safety had increased the effect of the water in the engine room and they all held onto something as the up angle approached fifteen, then twenty.

"Give safety another shot!" the ensign called down the hatch. When the air hit they began to ascend with a discernible rush, pointing up at twenty-five degrees by the conning tower clinometer. Their feet lost traction on the deck and they moved by using their arms.

"Distance to the fish?"

"Three hunnert! She is hanging on, she is—"

"Control! Blow the after group! I want to come up as flat as I can. As soon as we broach, open safety vent."

"Aye, aye!" the chief called and as the air hit the after group the stern lifted and some of the up angle began to come off.

"Sprague, when we pass seventy feet, put the number one scope up and put me on his generated bearing. Tell tubes forward to stand by. Open number two outer door."

The ensign went to the TDC and studied the solution generating. He only needed one final check bearing. He could fire with what he had now in the TDC, but he only had one torpedo left and when that was gone—nothing. There was no way to be sure the solution was correct without the final bearing on the target.

"One hunnert yards on the fish!" Chekenian shouted.

"All stop!" the ensign said. The scope slithered up from the well and the ensign turned and squatted down on the deck and when the eyepiece cleared the deck locked his face to it and rode it up. He did this in one graceful, unthinking motion, as if he had been born to command a submarine in combat.

"Blow all main ballast!" he cried, glued to the scope, watching immaculate bluegreen water begin to churn and bubble, the light gathering now, focusing into his right eye through the powerful optics in the tall steel tube until with a final shimmer the head broke clear and the entire surface of the sea stood revealed to him pristine and brilliant, sunstruck and endless, everything there but too much to see through one eye and the cumbersome periscope mechanism. Through the tail of his eye he caught a clue, swung toward it, and was looking into water again.

"Control! Blow safety dry! Keep me up! *There he is!* I

can see his whole conning tower! *You're dunking me, goddam it*—there. Final bearing and shoot! Stand by— *mark it!*"

Sprague read the periscope bearing and called it out. The ensign went to the TDC and matched the bearing and called out, "Set! Shoot!" and Sprague hit the firing key and shouted into the phone, "Fire two!"

"She's away!" Chekenian said. "Hot, straight, and norm—"

"The tin can!" the ensign cried, swinging the scope. "Coming right down our starboard beam. The son of a bitch is going to ram us. Sound the collision alarm! *Sound the collision a*—"

There was a terrific explosion close aboard. The ensign saw the destroyer elevate in the middle as if a gigantic hand had lifted it, then it broke in two with a yellow ball of flame, both halves burning. He could see human figures in the air and some sliding down the sides, burning.

"Holy Christ!" the ensign said. "Somebody sank the can. I don't—"

"The fish—" Chekenian said.

"Ours?"

"The acoustic fish," Sprague said. "That destroyer's screws. It must have shifted to the tin can's screws when we stopped ours."

"But what about the Mark 14?"

"Still running!" Chekenian said. "Steam fish? Still running h, s, and n!"

"Swing back around," Sprague said. The ensign was already swinging.

"How much time left for the torpedo run?" he said.

"Well," Sprague said, "if the submarine is where we figured him—"

"Goddam it, he's right there. I'm looking right—oh oh.

Oh, Jesus. He's seen us! He must have been looking at that can and he's seen us. He's turning toward. He is diving! He is heading this way and diving. That bastard is going to get a—"

The explosion came instantly, like another depth charge, lifting the deck beneath them abruptly, then dropping it to wallow crazily. But there was no one there to depth-charge them now. They realized what it was.

"You hit him!" Sprague cried. "You hit the son of a bitch!" He was holding onto the wheel with the helmsman.

Chekenian was howling, dancing around, holding his other ear. The ensign was flat on his back, his face numb and thick where the eyepiece had struck him. He struggled to his feet and tried to look through the periscope but his right eye was swollen shut. He jammed his left eye against the eyepiece. His viewpoint was terrifically elevated and swaying now and he saw that they were on the surface, rolling and pitching heavily in the turbulence caused by the two explosions. He saw the other submarine's stern angling surreally in the air, propellers spinning. Then she went straight down, not a dive but a sickening plunge and shortly there was another explosion which bounced the deck beneath them wildly.

"We can't hold her up!" the chief called. "She is starting to slip."

"Keep her on the surface if you can!"

"Forward engine room reports they are abandoning the compartment," Sprague said. "And after battery reports flooding and short circuits."

"Lost hydraulic power!" a planesman called.

The lights went out. "Lost electrical power," Sprague said. "Christ, we've lost everything!"

"She is settling!" the chief of the watch called.

"Blow safety and negative dry!" the ensign shouted. "Keep the blow going in the main ballast. Open the blows up and leave 'em. Blow bow buoyancy. Pass the word to abandon ship through all hatches. Make sure everybody is out of the flooded compartments, and close the doors."

Sprague called every compartment on the sound powered phone. The ensign depressed the periscope and looked at the foredeck. The hatch popped open and men began coming up out of the forward torpedo room. He swung around and looked aft. Men were leaving from the after battery, the after engine room, the after torpedo room hatches.

"We'll have close to neutral buoyancy for a while anyway," the ensign said. "She is sinking, but it'll take a little while." The decks were just awash now. He looked over his shoulder at Chekenian.

"Chief, we are going to abandon. Get out." But the old chief just stared at him, his hands over his ears.

"Come on, for God's sake, let's get out," Sprague said. He was undogging the upper hatch.

"Get Chekenian. He can't hear anything."

The ensign noticed that the last man out of each hatch was reflexively shutting it behind him, a habit so long ingrained it could not be ignored even now. A slight film of water covered the hatches now. She was sinking but she was taking her time with safety and the main ballast blown. The internal hemorrhaging would kill her, but there were some minutes left yet.

Looking away from the bright dazzle of the scope into the dim conning tower made it very difficult to see. It took a while to understand that Sprague still stood on the ladder to the upper hatch, his hands over his head, and Chekenian stood just by the sonar, staring.

"Sprague!" the ensign called. "God damn it, Sprague,

take Chekenian and get the hell off. I am trying to find the captain and Burt Foster. They didn't leave forward and they didn't leave aft."

But Sprague had retreated into open-mouthed immobility, staring at the lower hatch from which an incredible apparition was emerging into the ambient gloom.

At first it seemed a ghost, a hallucination, and the ensign doubted his eyes. Then Sprague got the battle lantern switched on.

In the flat white glare of the single battle lantern a white officer's hat floated up atop a sea of bandages inexpertly applied. As they stared the bandages gave way to a dress blue service uniform which gained the deck a hand an arm and finally a leg at a time until a form familiar but still unbelievable stood unsteadily before them.

It was the captain, Orin Feldman, standing before them in his dress blue lieutenant commander's uniform with medals and sword and wearing his gray inspection gloves.

"Captain—" the ensign said.

"Orin," Sprague said. "What—"

Neither of them moved. Someone else was coming up the hatch. It was the steward, carrying Feldman's boat cloak and briefcase. He stood for a moment blinking into the lantern and their concerted stare.

"I bandage best I could," Martinez said. "Mr. Foster and me—he make us dress him up and he want to come up here."

"What for?" the ensign said.

"Court-martial," Feldman said, his voice weak and fuzzy through the layers of white gauze. "My fault." He saluted, the gray glove marooned in the air unable to find the hat visor which now sat crookedly off to one side. Jacqueline must have pinned the medals on for some cere-

mony long ago; they formed a neatly overlapped row at
his breast, glinting dully in the light.

"Captain—" the ensign said.

"My fault, sir," Feldman said. "All my fault."

Martinez tapped his forehead and moved his forefinger
in a little circle, rolling his eyes.

"Yeah," Sprague said.

"Get him up and over," the ensign snapped.

"Aye, aye, Captain," Sprague said. "Come on Orin . . ."

He started him up the ladder to the upper hatch, the
helmsman and Chekenian guiding him, Martinez following with briefcase and flowing cloak, Feldman moving
with surprising sureness over terrain literally engraved
in his brain.

"Martinez," the ensign said, "where is Mr. Foster now?"

The steward shrugged, took his hand off the ladder,
tapped his temple again and made the same motion. "Was
sitting in wardroom, having cup of coffee." He went on up.

"Come on," Sprague said. "Let's get out." Sunlight was
coming in and the strange sweet smell of fresh sea air.

"You go ahead. See that the captain is all right, take
care of the captain."

"You're the captain. Come on."

"Go ahead. Take care of things up there. That's an
order."

Sprague looked at him. Then he went on up the ladder
and out the hatch.

The ensign climbed down through the lower hatch and
down the ladder. Control room was empty, eerie and
haunted in the light from the battle lanterns. The valves
on the air manifold were all wide open. The unending hiss
of high-pressure air seemed like a ghostly scream. He saw
that the watertight door to forward battery was shut. As
he worked the dogs he realized how badly his right arm

and shoulder were hurt. He did as much of the work as he could with his left arm. He left the door carefully open behind him. The water was not yet up to the bottom of the coaming.

The forward battery compartment was dry, the long, dark passageway broken only by light from a battle lantern spilling from the door of the captain's stateroom.

"Hello, Burt."

"Oh, hi, Junior. Guess you better be getting your ass ashore." He squinted over at the depth gauge.

"Might say the same for you, Burt. But you don't look like you intend to go anywhere."

"This is my home, kid. Where it goes, I go. I don't want no dramatic horsecock from you, neither."

The mustang was lying on the captain's bunk, his head propped up on the pillow, the captain's bottle of scotch on the open writing desk within easy reach, a cigar in his hand, an ash tray tidily on his stomach. He was wearing his old frayed bathrobe and his carpet slippers. On his head was his ancient stained chief's hat.

"This isn't your room," the ensign said. "Your bunk is across the hall."

They studied each other. The mustang's moonface broke into a crooked grin. "Now you wouldn't order me out on a technicality, would you, kid? I mean I always wanted to command my own boat, I figure this is the last chanct I'll ever get. Anyway, time like this, a fella wants a room to hisself. You understand."

"I understand, Burt."

"You won't tell no one and get me into trouble?"

"Well, I dunno. I can't make any promises. You might get put in hack."

"Tsk tsk. You always was a little horseshit trouble-maker, wasn't you?"

"I don't know. Was I?"

They smiled at each other, then they both looked at the depth gauge at the foot of the bunk. Nothing described the Navy more specifically to the ensign than that depth gauge at the foot of the bunk where the captain could see it just by raising his head.

"Like a drink, kid?"

"Yeah. Sure." He took the bottle, took a drink, coughed, handing it back.

"Something I came across under the pillow, Jimmie boy. If you hadn't come by I would of kept 'em, don't know exactly why. No good to me. Guess you ought to have them."

He handed the ensign a pair of black nylon panties, neatly folded.

"Tell her good-by for me, Junior. I never got to know her. Always wanted to, no, no, take that look off your face, nothing like that. Just talk to her and maybe joke around and all, the way the others always did. I was always afraid of her. You know? Like I might get her dirty if I touched her or even spoke to her. Tell her something nice about me. That inboard valve, I had that fixed real good, for a while anyway. Oh, almost forgot. One more thing. There's a big brown envelope on the wardroom table over there. For you, I guess, since you're in command."

"Message for the captain?"

"From the squadron commodore. Hand-delivered. Says this whole screwy operation has been called off."

"What do you mean, called off?"

"By CNO hisself. Too risky. President got wind of it or something, Murphy figured. Anyway, says they are sending a destroyer out to escort that commie sub that was in trouble."

"One of our own destroyers?"

"Well, they wouldn't send somebody else's out, would they? They sent the old *Everly*. Spunky Waters' new command. It's all wrote down in there."

"You read it?"

"Murphy did. He told me about it."

"Then that was Spunky Waters' destroyer up there?"

"No. You would have known if it was."

"How?"

"He would of sent you the code word, the recognition signal—fugaroo or something."

"Figaro."

"Yeah. So Murphy told you."

"But why did they send that down by messenger if they knew we were getting underway?"

"We wasn't the only action addressees. The commodore didn't want to let out what we was up to by trying to stop us, so he sent this message to every submarine operating out of Key West: that that commie submarine was being escorted by the *Everly* until she could be handed over to some commie surface ship to help her home."

"But why a recognition signal if—"

"That's the clever part. The squadron commodore is very clever. Or CNO is. Because lately our nukes has been being sunk by some mysterious unknown submarine. So to protect this commie nuke from that unknown submarine, the *Everly* was escorting her and if any submarine was detected in the area, why the *Everly* would flash FIGARO at him or send it on the sonar, and if it was one of our own boats it would immediately surface or if on the surface flash back its own name."

"And if it didn't?"

"Then obviously it was the mysterious unknown submarine that had been sinking our nukes. And probably going to attack. So the *Everly* would have to sink it to protect the nuke she was escorting."

The ensign looked at the depth gauge. They were already well under here in the stateroom. The water would be approaching the upper conning tower hatch soon.

"That message went to all submarines in the Key West area?" the ensign said.

"Yeah."

"So if anything happened to that commie submarine—"

"It would have had to be the unknown enemy submarine that done it."

"I see. Yes. That's the way it would look."

"Ain't the Navy I joined no more. Bunch of kids like you. Fifty-knot submarines. Shit. Who wants all that shit?"

"Wait a minute. How did Murphy know all this?"

"I just told you. He sat right over there and read the papers in that brown envelope."

"When?"

"How should I know when? Just before we dove for the first time, I guess. Why?"

"So he knew all along."

"I don't know what he knew or didn't know when, but I know this. He is out of all this, but you ain't. He don't have to live with all this, but you do. So tell me."

"Tell you what?"

"How you going to do it?"

"You know how deep it is here, Burt?"

"No, but I'll find out right there." He indicated the depth gauge with his cigar, tapped the ashes neatly into the ash tray on his big stomach.

"It's over a thousand feet. You'll never get out."

"You really think I'm planning on that, kid?"

"No—but—ahhh hell. I don't know much about anything any more."

"So you are finally growing up. You'll be an admiral yet.
Good one, too, like your old man. Me, they're going to retire me next year anyhow, then what? Some old sailors'
home or something? People come and stare at you, feed
you things, like animals in the zoo, and bring you presents
while you get all them old man's diseases one after another and they stick you and cut you and patch you up
for the next one, fuck it. You got about a minute till the
conning tower hatch goes under, kid."

"Burt, you old bastard—"

"Know something, kid? As smartass Academy pukes go,
you ain't so bad."

"—I'm going to miss you."

"Yeah? Come out here on your yacht any old time. I'll
only be a thousand feet away. Fat, dumb, and happy. Go
on now. Close the back door when you leave. I don't want
to get my feet wet, might catch cold . . ."

The mustang's laughter echoed as the ensign stepped
through the watertight door at the after end of the compartment. Water was just beginning to come over the
coaming. He dogged it hard and, hurrying now, splashed
through the control room. The boat was down by the
stern and as he moved aft through the compartment it got
deeper, up to his waist as he found the ladder. But he
didn't go up.

He stood immobile in the ghostly control room, listening to the diminishing hiss of the high-pressure air. The
air banks were depleting fast now. Half walking, half
swimming, he thrashed to the control manifold in the
forward port corner of the compartment. He found the
main ballast tank vents, threw them to the open position,

then, splashing furiously, made his way to the ladder and up.

The long swell was sending water into the upper hatch now, but it was not yet a steady stream. He had to fight a little, but not very much. Then it became a surprisingly easy transition. He simply climbed up the ladder to the bridge deck, climbed up on the step to the turtleback, and then just stood there as the water climbed slowly up his legs.

The submarine was gaining negative buoyancy now but she seemed reluctant to leave the surface for good. There was no turbulence, no suction, she just drifted very slowly and deliberately down, air bubbling up from the ballast tanks frothy and festive in the bright sparkling sunshine, the long dark shape of the hull clearly visible as it sank with stately grace, a fantastic sight in the translucent water.

He watched the conning tower fairwater go under. The number one periscope, still raised, slowly submerged, canting slightly aft, until finally he was swimming in the open ocean looking into the blank periscope eye just level with him, then it too disappeared. The ensign felt rent, felt a tearing frustration, the sea above, the sparkling wavetops, ships in the middle distance, yachts cruising peacefully this way and that keeping clear of the naval maneuvers, an airplane circling, Navy ships with white bow waves and signal flags snapping, sea birds climbing, soaring, and below, dwindling now into darkness, the submarine, shimmering and vague now, dreamlike, drifting gently away.

Then some delicate balance was disturbed, negative buoyancy assumed with a rush. She took a big up angle and just slid away backward into the infinite deep. The last he saw of her was her bow, the bowplanes the sonar-dome the lines where the superstructure met the pressure hull giving her a vaguely human look. She seemed to be smiling. Then a sailor had his arm and he was being hauled into a gray Navy boat, Orin Feldman seated in the stern sheets in his boat cloak and bandages and sword.

16

ENEMY SUB SUNK!

SANK OUR NUCLEAR SUBS, SAYS NAVY

Sinks Three Vessels in Vicious Attack!

NATIONALITY UNKNOWN

Not Russian, Navy Says

PRESIDENT TO ADDRESS NATION

Ensign Hero

The rear admiral read the front-page story carefully, following it to the inside pages where there were related stories.

USS EVERLY, DEVILFISH AND RUSSIAN
SUBMARINE SUNK BY MYSTERY SUB IN
SAVAGE BATTLE OFF KEY WEST

ENSIGN IS NAVAL HERO IN DARING COUNTERATTACK

Sinks Mystery Sub

SAVES NATION FROM DISASTER

Navy In Uproar Over Certain Irregularities On U.S. Sub

Captain Shell Shocked

Loses Ship

·

"Shell-shocked," the rear admiral said. "Haven't heard that term since the First World War."

"That's quite a headline for the New York *Times*, Admiral," the aide said. "They usually don't run them that big for anything less than a war."

"This was a war," the admiral said. "In fact it may be a prototype for—saaay, look at that. Picture of my boy. You see that? From the Academy yearbook. So stern and proper. And young."

"Sir, it's time for the briefing."

The aide fell in step as the rear admiral swept out of his office and walked along the E ring.

"Congratulations, Admiral."

"Thanks. The boy did all right, didn't he?"

"Yessir. But I meant on your selection for vice admiral."

"Oh? Do we have some official word on that?"

"The operation was obviously a success. Everybody knows that's all they were waiting for."

"Well, I won't order any new uniforms just yet."

The rear admiral nodded curtly to a passing group of naval officers who were staring and whispering among themselves.

"Too bad about Commodore Forbes," the aide said. "The *Post* says he is being court-martialed."

"Well, he was squadron commodore. Any irregularities aboard that boat, he's responsible."

"One of those columnists in there is pretty nasty about the commodore being used as a scapegoat for the higher-ups."

"Well that columnist happens to be wrong again, and as a matter of fact, so is the *Post*. I just talked to Forbes on the phone and he has decided to retire."

"Under fire like that, Admiral? Wouldn't it look—"

"Commander, if you would like to write your own column you are free to do so. Hanson Baldwin is Naval Academy class of '24 and he is doing very well with the

New York *Times*. He resigned his commission of course. You might want to give him a call."

"Sir, I didn't mean—"

"Oh, check my calendar, will you? Make sure I am cleared for the rest of the day. That's all."

In the office of the Chief of Naval Operations was a select group of senators, senior admirals, and some highly placed civilians from D.O.D. and the White House. They were drinking coffee and reading the morning papers, speaking in somber tones.

When the rear admiral walked in, CNO stood up to greet him and shake his hand. Some of the others stood up, and there was scattered applause, but about as many remained seated in pointed silence.

"Gentlemen," CNO said, and the rear admiral could not remember ever hearing that peculiar nervous edge in his voice. But then the rear admiral had never seen CNO before in the presence of men who were, in some ways at least, his senior in the chain of command.

"I don't need to introduce Jim Hillerby to most of you," CNO was saying. "He is the brains behind the operation. He conceived it, planned it, and carried it out."

CNO then stepped away from the rear admiral with a certain definite motion which the rear admiral tried not to interpret.

He stood looking at them and made them watch him insert a cigarette in his ivory holder and very carefully get it lighted. Then he explained the entire operation from start to finish.

"As you know, and the President will emphasize this tonight, the Russian government has expressed official gratitude that the threat to the under-water security of both our navies has been removed. And our governments have exchanged condolences vis-à-vis the mutual loss of vessels in this action to an unknown enemy."

"But how about the crew of the *Devilfish?*" an admiral from SACLant said.

"There are no constraints whatsoever upon any of the crew, sir. They are at liberty to talk to anybody about anything and at any length."

"Isn't that rather dangerous?" a senator said.

"You may recall, Senator, that Admiral Dan Gallery suggested something similar in connection with our men taken prisoner of war in Korea. To keep them from being tortured to divulge information they didn't have anyway. His advice was never made policy, but I think it had considerable merit. It's especially pertinent in a submarine, where only the skipper really sees what is going on. If you read those stories in your morning papers carefully you will note that so far one sailor says the *Devilfish* was definitely attacked by a nuclear submarine, another sailor says the battle involved at least a dozen ships and some aircraft, and still another says there were no other ships out there at all. Incidentally, we are going to give them a choice of an honorable discharge or a chance to ship over with a fresh start and a clean record."

"And the ensign?" an admiral from CincLant said.

"Yes," a senator said. "What about him?"

"We thought you would like to meet him. I'm looking forward to this myself, I haven't seen him yet either. Just a few words on the phone yesterday after they hauled him ashore." He looked over at CNO. "Admiral, would you be good enough to have him brought in now, please?"

"Isn't he with you? He isn't here."

"Why, no, sir. When he didn't show up I just naturally assumed you'd had him brought directly to your office."

"Well, goddammit," CNO said. "We better check on this." His aide jumped up and went to the outer office.

There was some murmuring and one of the civilians from D.O.D. said, "Damn cute trick, hiding the kid."

"Maybe he's been misfiled," one of the admirals said, and there was laughter, not particularly friendly.

"Look here," the man from the White House staff said. "Everything seems to hinge on this kid ensign. What's wrong with him? Is he shell-shocked too? I mean he'd have to be crazy to do what he did anyway—"

"Gentlemen, gentlemen," CNO said. "Admiral Hillerby is not trying to hide him, I am sure. We thought he was here, waiting. Just a small confusion. We'll clear it up quickly, won't we, Jim?"

"I certainly hope—yes, *sir*—just a matter of—well, gentlemen, we should take a minute or so while we are, uh, waiting to discuss the identify of the, uh, putative third submarine in the battle, the mysterious submarine supposedly sunk by the *Devilfish* after it had sunk the others. It obviously could not have been Russian since it sank a Russian sub along with our destroyer. If it was not Russian, what was it?

"Well, the most popular answer, as you've read in your newspapers and some of you probably saw the 'Today' show this morning, is Chinese. But I imagine that will change if our relations with China improve and some of the other suggestions will be considered more seriously: Egyptian, Transylvanian, God knows what all. Meanwhile, of course, we keep looking for the wreckage which in water that deep will never be found."

"Scuse me, Admiral," an aide said. "There is some ensign out here claims he is—would you be good enough to take a look at him, sir?"

They had not recognized him in the outer office because

he just did not look like a junior officer coming to a high-level briefing in the Pentagon.

"Jimmie?" the rear admiral said. "For God's sake, is that you?"

The ensign's right arm was in a black sling, and the side of his face was bruised and swollen, the right eye reduced to a narrow slit. He was not wearing any kind of a dress uniform—no glove, no sword, no decoration, no polished golden button or shiny mark of rank. He wore working khaki, clean and heavily starched, which gave him a rather dashing look among all the heavy serge and gabardine in the offices, and a black tie of nonregulation knit, loosely knotted.

His shoes were dark brown pebble grain brogues, and on his head was a hat salt-stained and watersplotched, the gold braid already mostly turned green.

Since he wore neither collar marks nor blouse, he looked like a young chief petty officer who had been in a fight and won as a prize an ancient officer's hat. He was smoking casually a slim cigar.

"Hi, Dad."

"But you said you were perfectly all right!"

"I was attacked by a periscope eyepiece"—grinning, which closed the eye completely, as they walked on in.

The rear admiral kept interrupting, trying to answer the questions asked of the ensign.

"Admiral Hillerby," the man from the White House staff said. "Would you please let the ensign speak for himself?"

The ensign told it all again, but this time with firsthand detail and a certain calm authority that kept most of his audience leaning forward in their chairs.

"Then she went down. There were a lot of ships and they took us back to Key West. The captain is in the hospital and I've been to see him. They are operating today and they say chances aren't good, but not quite hopeless. I told you about the two officers we lost, and as acting CO I am recommending the Medal of Honor for both of them. I am also recommending the Navy Cross for Captain Feldman and two of my enlisted men, the quartermaster and the chief sonarman."

"And he brought them both here with him to meet you," the rear admiral said, consulting a piece of paper. "Chief Chekenian, and Quartermaster First Class Sprague. He has recommended that Sprague be promoted to chief, and we have a new chief's hat for him." He signaled an aide who produced the cardboard hatbox.

"Sprague didn't make it, sir," the ensign said, moving to the door to the outer office where he shouted, "Chekenian! *In here!*" beckoning, and the old chief came in in his blue uniform with red hashmarks up to the elbow. It was the uniform he had been swimming in, and it had shrunk. His wrists hung down and the trousers exposed bony ankles in stockings neatly held up by garters, and waterlogged and puffy black shoes. One ear was stuffed with a large wad of cotton, the other was covered with a bandage. His weathered face wore already the steady sweet smile of the deaf and he watched carefully the ensign's lips.

"Chekenian spent the night in the infirmary at the naval station and these were the only clothes he had. I stayed with a friend and was able to borrow a change of khaki and some shoes. All my stuff went down with the boat. We didn't have a chance to get to a uniform shop before the plane left. We were trying to find Sprague. That's what we held up the plane for, why we're late. We're still trying to track him down by telephone."

There were a lot of questions about tactical detail from

the admirals, which the ensign answered crisply. He was properly subordinate but very firm and when an admiral with dolphins over his ribbons began to argue a point of submarine seamanship, the ensign more than held his own.

Then the man from the White House staff got up and said, "Ensign, how would you like to be on television tonight with the President of the United States?"

"We appreciate the thought," the rear admiral said. "But really he is very tired, been through an awful lot and—"

"Admiral, let the ensign speak for himself."

"What do I have to do?" the ensign said, fishing another slim cigar out of his pocket, leaning to accept a light from a blue sleeve heavy with gold.

"Just stand there. Maybe say a paragraph or so along the lines you just did. We'll write it for you. Idiot cards. Nothing to worry about."

CNO was standing very close now, smiling benignly, his hand on the ensign's shoulder. "We'll get him spruced up, Jack. New suit of dress blues and—"

"No, no, just the way he is. Except for the cigar maybe . . ."

The meeting was breaking up, the important and distinguished gentlemen on their feet talking among themselves, some gathered around the ensign. An aide summoned CNO to the outer office for an important telephone call. CNO returned and drew the rear admiral aside, over toward his desk.

"Jim—I'm afraid it's bad news. The selection board. They are passing you over for promotion to vice admiral."

"But it *worked*—"

"The operation was a success. The objective was accomplished. But you stepped on too many toes, left too many people in the dark, skipped too many links in the chain of command, embarrassed too many VIPs. Private grumbling in Congress. Senior admirals threatening to resign. There is talk of a court-martial, but I think we can get them to settle for Forbes, and your being passed over."

"There wasn't any other way to do it."

"I am genuinely sorry. I did what I could."

"I'm sure you did, sir, but—"

"You have the satisfaction of knowing that you helped save the nation from disaster."

"Excuse me, Admiral," an aide said. "There is a lady outside claims she is with the ensign."

"Maybe Mary Beth," the rear admiral said. "What's she look like?"

The aide started to use his hands, gave it up as undignified. "Sexy, Admiral."

"That's not Mary Beth," the rear admiral said. He went over to the ensign. "Excuse me, Jim. You didn't bring a lady with you did you?"

"Yeah," the ensign said. "She's phoning about Sprague."

The admiral nodded and the aide brought her in. Her presence stopped all conversation in the room. She stood in her yellow dress as if in her own sunlight with her pale, luminous complexion, her strawcolored hair falling gently to her slim shoulders, the outline of her figure suggested through the silken fabric. Immaculate and cool, she shook CNO's hand, then the rear admiral's.

"You look surprised."

"Glad to see you, Jacqueline. I wasn't expecting you."

"Well, did you locate Sprague?" the ensign said.

"I had a devil of a time doing it. Talked to a bunch of bartenders. He apparently walked right from the waterfront to Duval Street, where he picked up some woman. Finally got the bartender at the Havana Madrid, who gave me a blow-by-blow description. He was fighting the Shore Patrol right then. That was five minutes ago."

"In the morning?"

"They tossed him out a couple of times last night. He came back."

"Where is he now?"

"Either in the hospital or jail. It was a car full of Shore Patrol with the civilian police on the way."

"Jesus, I've got to get right back," the ensign said.

"First thing in the morning," the rear admiral said.

"No, sir. Right now."

"You're forgetting your television appearance tonight.'

"What television appearance?" Jacqueline said.

"With the President of the United States."

"Is this Sprague the man you recommended for chief?" CNO said dryly.

"He'll be okay if I get back in time. He is very good at sea, but he can't handle the beach."

"On television with the *President?*" Jacqueline said.

"We'll have somebody take care of him," the rear admiral said. "We'll call the base in Key West."

"No, sir. He's one of my men."

"Nobody else can do anything with him," Jacqueline said. "We've got to get back right now. Maybe the President could make it some other time."

"Now, *wait*—you are still an ensign in the Navy, Jim. I can order you to stay here."

"Yessir, and you can court-martial me for insubordination. But I am going back to get Sprague under control before he gets into something none of us can get him out of. And the others too, the rest of the crew, they'll need a lot of help getting relocated. Paperwork, clothes, money, housing, they need an officer there that knows them. Most of them are going to ship over."

"He's right," CNO said. "An officer's first duty is to his men."

"But my God, Admiral," the rear admiral said. "The President of the United States—the *Commander in Chief—*"

"Admiral," the man from the White House staff said. "It wasn't the President yet. It was just my idea and maybe the President wouldn't have bought it anyway. Ensign, I admire your spunk. Give me a call sometime." He left and then all the visitors had gone.

"Well, Jim," the rear admiral said. "I don't know what to make of you."

"Ensign Hillerby," CNO said, "we were going to make a big thing of this, ceremony, all our distinguished guests watching, little speech and all, but things don't always work out just the way you expect. I can't approve the decorations all by myself, we need a little time for that, congressional approval, you understand. But I can certainly make a spot promotion, and you are now a lieutenant, junior grade." He was holding a small plastic box in which were two shiny silver bars. He handed it to Jacqueline. "Would you do the honors?"

"Wait a minute," the ensign said.

"Now, damn it, Jim!" the rear admiral said. "Don't tell me you are going to refuse—what the hell has got—"

"No, sir," the ensign said, grinning, digging in his trouserpocket. "Nothing like that. Every young man likes to get ahead in his chosen profession." He produced a handful of small change, car keys, a book of matches. "Jackie, look in my other pocket."

"For what?"

"Just pull it all out. There. Use those."

She brought up two bars, once silver, now tarnished mostly green.

"Foster's," he said.

"What?" the rear admiral said.

"Our mustang j.g.," the ensign said. "Went down with the boat. Trapped while throwing the main battery disconnects, saved us all."

"Oh, yes, yes, of course, you told us about him."

Jacqueline was pinning the tarnished bars on the crisp collarpoints. She kissed him.

"We are doing this all haphazard," the rear admiral said. "We had planned—well. I had a little speech all—" He was removing the gold dolphins from his chest. He stepped to the ensign, hesitated.

"Jacqueline, he'd probably prefer that you do this too, but I'd like to indulge myself. I have spoken with Commodore Forbes about the status of your progress toward Qualification, Jim. Been approved all along the line and entered in your official record. I saw to it myself. Want you to wear my dolphins. Now you are *officially* a submariner. I hope someday you will pin them on your own son's chest."

Abruptly there were tears in the rear admiral's eyes which he brushed quickly away, clearing his throat noisily, patting the ensign on the shoulder. The dolphins were an old and burnished gold against the crisp khaki shirt.

"We'll have the plane take you back right now, if that's what you want. It might as well wait for you."

"I wouldn't see any point in waiting, sir. I've got next-of-kin letters to write—Murphy had a mother, and Foster had family somewhere, it's in their records. And I told the destroyer commodore I wanted to help out with the letters to the *Everly* wives. And some of the *Devilfish* sailors want me to write next-of-kin letters to their wives."

"The survivors?"

The ensign smiled. "We promised them a new start with a clean record."

"Why—I'm not sure that's legal. You better ask the admiral—"

CNO smiled, holding up his hands. "I don't want to know a thing about it."

"And we have to find a place to stay, big enough to take good care of Orin when he can come home."

"Oh, honey," Jacqueline said, "I meant to tell you. I got a line on a nice place not far from the hospital. Two bedrooms—"

"Where?" the rear admiral said.

"Out by the bridge to—"

"On Key West?"

"Sure," the ensign said.

"But I told you on the phone. You're all lined up for nuclear-power school. You'll be living in Bainbridge. You don't want a house in Key West right now."

"Dad, I appreciate all you have done about that. But I want to finish out my first sea-duty tour right where I am, in the boats. Commodore Forbes has promised as his last official act to assign me to another diesel boat operating out of Key West. When that's behind me then I'll put in for nuclear-power school like everybody else, and they can look at my record instead of my ancestry."

"It might not be quite that simple," CNO said. "You're a national figure now, some say a hero, but heroes have a way of being forgotten and even resented. Some pretty powerful people think you're not a hero at all but a troublemaker with bad judgment, that you should have surfaced at once and come back in, saved everybody all this upset—"

"And left the problem unsolved."

"That's what a lot of people like to do with problems, Jim. Keep putting them off, hoping they'll go away."

"This one would have turned into World War III."

"I know that, Jim. And your father knows that. I hope to God you will remember it in the years ahead. Because if you don't let your father and me help you now, we won't be able to do it later. When you walk out that door, you'll be just another j.g. in the fleet."

When the new j.g. didn't say anything, CNO said, "I think we've kept you long enough. We all have to get back to work." He stuck out his hand, the sleeve heavy with thick bands of gold.

The j.g. shook hands left-handed, then put on his salt-stained hat and saluted left-handed. The tarnished silver bars at his collar were greenish against the clean faded khaki, the dolphins a rich gold. The two admirals gravely returned the salute, though neither was covered.

"Where did you say you got the clean khaki?" the rear admiral said.

"At the motel. It was Murphy's."

"I see," the rear admiral said, glancing down. "And the shoes too?"

"Yes, sir. It's all a little big, but it's close enough."

"Close enough," the rear admiral said.

"Fair winds and a following sea, Lieutenant," CNO said.

Then they were leaving, making their way through the outer office, detained here and there by various officials shaking the new j.g.'s hand, wanting to meet the shapely lady in the yellow dress, so cool and self-contained, and behind them the old chief in his shrunken blue uniform bearing the new chief's hat in its cardboard box, his eyes fixed on the young submarine officer.